FAST HANDS

Fargo's keen eyes saw the move and recognized it for what it was—a trick. The man's hand closed around the butt of his pistol and jerked it from his belt.

Fargo fired first, but the man wasn't acting like he was injured now. Instead, he threw himself to the side with surprising speed, so that Fargo's slug went harmlessly past him. The gun in his hand roared, sending a bullet sizzling by Fargo's ear. He flung himself backward, diving to the ground and rolling into the shelter of the big rock from which he had tackled the bald man.

A bullet smacked into the rock and sent dust and stone shards showering down around Fargo. He spotted the bald man hurrying toward some trees on the riverbank and triggered a fast shot. It clipped the bald man's leg and sent him tumbling off his feet with a pained yelp.

Fargo saw the pistol fly through the air as the man dropped it. With a lithe motion, the Trailsman uncoiled from the ground and stalked forward, keeping his revolver trained on the fallen man.

"You . . . bastard," the dying man grated.

THE TRAILSMAN

#269

DEVIL'S DEN

by

Jon Sharpe

A SIGNET BOOK

SIGNET
Published by New American Library, a division of
Penguin Group (USA) Inc., 375 Hudson Street,
New York, New York 10014, U.S.A.
Penguin Books Ltd, 80 Strand,
London WC2R 0RL, England
Penguin Books Australia Ltd, 250 Camberwell Road,
Camberwell, Victoria 3124, Australia
Penguin Books Canada Ltd, 10 Alcorn Avenue,
Toronto, Ontario, Canada M4V 3B2
Penguin Books (N.Z.) Ltd, Cnr Rosedale and Airborne Roads,
Albany, Auckland 1310, New Zealand

Penguin Books Ltd, Registered Offices:
80 Strand, London WC2R 0RL, England

First published by Signet, an imprint of New American Library,
a division of Penguin Group (USA) Inc.

First Printing, March 2004
10   9   8   7   6   5   4   3   2   1

The first chapter of this book originally appeared in *New Mexico Nymph*, the
two hundred sixty-eighth volume in this series.

The Trailsman

Beginnings . . . they bend the tree and they mark the man. Skye Fargo was born when he was eighteen. Terror was his midwife, vengeance his first cry. Killing spawned Skye Fargo, ruthless, cold-blooded murder. Out of the acrid smoke of gunpowder still hanging in the air, he rose, cried out a promise never forgotten.

The Trailsman they began to call him all across the West: searcher, scout, hunter, the man who could see where others only looked, his skills for hire but not his soul, the man who lived each day to the fullest, yet trailed each tomorrow. Skye Fargo, the Trailsman, the seeker who could take the wildness of a land and the wanting of a woman and make them his own.

Indian Territory, 1860—
Where evil men brew bad whiskey
and worse trouble.

Skye Fargo knew he was being followed.

The big man in buckskins didn't turn around in the saddle to study his back trail, but he knew somebody was there. His lake-blue eyes narrowed as he felt the skin crawl in the middle of his back, as if someone were drawing a bead on the spot. He kept the Ovaro moving steadily, varying the pace every now and then just to confirm his suspicions.

Better to draw the follower on for a spell, he thought. Bide his time and wait for the right moment to turn the tables on whoever it was. Assuming, of course, that nobody bushwhacked him first.

Whoever was back there, he sure as hell knew how to spoil a beautiful day, Fargo told himself.

If there was one thing the Trailsman appreciated—besides a pretty woman, an honest poker game, and a glass of good whiskey, that is—it was nice weather. He had spent most of his life dealing with extreme heat and cold, droughts and floods, sandstorms and snowstorms. A day such as today, with clear blue skies, warm sunshine, and a cool breeze, was something to be savored.

He had followed the Arkansas River westward toward Fort Smith for several days and expected to reach the town before night fell again. Mountains rose to the north and south of the river valley—some of them rounded and covered with trees, others rockier and rising to craggy peaks. Spring was far enough along so that wildflowers bloomed in some of the meadows, perfuming the air with their scent. Fargo was the sort of man who could find beauty in nature no matter where he was, but a fella didn't have to look very hard for it around here.

Too bad a serpent had made its way into this Eden. Fargo figured the man trailing him was up to no good. Otherwise, he would have announced himself before now.

Still following the river, Fargo rode around a sharp bend in the stream, and past a large boulder. This was the spot, he sensed immediately. He sent the big black-and-white stallion off the road and into the trees that covered the hillside on his left.

Fargo swung down from the saddle and led the Ovaro deeper into the woods. He tied the reins around the trunk of a tree and then hurried back toward the river and the boulder that loomed next to the road. Fargo climbed part of the way up the rugged chunk of rock and crouched there, out of sight of the trail.

He waited with the innate patience of a born frontiersman until he heard the steady beat of a horse's hooves on the road. The animal and its rider drew even with the boulder and started past it. Fargo scrambled the rest of the way to the top and found himself looking down on the rider's broad-brimmed black hat. He dived off the boulder and made a flying tackle.

His arms went around the man on horseback and tore him out of the saddle. With a wild, startled cry, the man fell, landing hard on the ground with Fargo on top of him. The impact knocked the breath out of the man. He lay there gasping for air as Fargo rolled to the side and then came up, drawing his Colt.

Fargo didn't know the man, though there was something vaguely familiar about him. He was burly and bald, with bushy muttonchop whiskers on his face. His rough clothing showed a lot of wear. He had an old pistol tucked behind his belt.

The man started to push himself upright, but the sight of Fargo's Colt—trained on him—made him freeze. "Just rest easy, friend," Fargo said in a flinty voice that wasn't friendly at all. "Who are you, and why have you been following me?"

A sullen look came over the man's face as he propped himself on his elbow and rubbed his jaw. "Are you crazy, mister?" he whined. "I don't know you. Why'd you jump me?"

"You've been riding behind me all afternoon."

"Well, hell, is it a crime for a fella to ride along a road? That's what it's there for!"

"You slowed down every time I slowed down," Fargo pointed out, "and you rode faster every time I did. But you always stayed just far enough back so that if I turned around, you could duck into the trees and not be spotted. That's what you thought, anyway."

"I don't know what the hell you're talkin'—" The man stopped short, and Fargo saw the determination to continue the argument go out of him. The man said, "I told Barker it was a mistake. You can't go followin' the damn Trailsman without him catchin' on."

Fargo gestured with the barrel of the Colt. "Get up, and tell me who Barker is. Did the two of you plan to rob me?"

The man climbed laboriously to his feet. He still seemed to be a little shaky from being knocked off his horse. He passed his hand across his eyes and swayed slightly. "Barker's just a fella I met a few days ago in Dardenelle. Don't know why he wanted to follow you. He never did say."

Dardenelle was a settlement to the east, also on the Arkansas River. Fargo had stayed at a hotel there the previous night. He wasn't surprised that that was where the mysterious Barker and this man—name still unknown—had spotted him. He hadn't made any secret of his presence—he'd eaten supper in the hotel dining room and had a few drinks in a tavern just down the street.

Fargo was on his way to Fort Smith in response to a message from an old friend. He wondered if his two followers had any connection with that situation.

And for that matter, where in blazes was Barker, anyway?

The man he had captured let out a groan and put both hands on his head. "I don't feel so good, Fargo," he complained. "I hit my head when you knocked me off my horse. Feels like I might've busted something. Ohhh . . ."

He staggered to the side, and as he did so, his right hand dropped from his head toward his waist. Fargo's keen eyes saw the move and recognized it for what it was—a trick. The man's hand now closed around the butt of his pistol and jerked it from behind his belt.

Fargo fired first, but the man wasn't acting like he was injured now. Instead, he threw himself to the side with surprising speed, so that Fargo's slug went harmlessly past him. The gun in his hand roared, sending a bullet sizzling by Fargo's ear.

Before Fargo could squeeze off a second shot, another gun blasted from somewhere nearby. That would be Barker, Fargo thought, as something tugged at the sleeve of his buckskin shirt. He flung himself backward, diving to the ground and rolling into the shelter of the big rock from which he had tackled the bald man.

A bullet smacked into the rock and sent dust and stone shards showering down around Fargo. He spotted the bald man hurrying toward some trees on the riverbank and triggered a fast shot. It clipped the bald man's leg and sent him tumbling off his feet with a pained yelp.

The sound of hoofbeats came from the road, back to the east. Fargo had the boulder between him and whoever was coming, probably Barker. He waited, with the Colt ready in his hand, but then the hoofbeats stopped abruptly. When they resumed a few seconds later, they were going in the other direction.

Barker must have changed his mind about continuing the attack. He was taking off for the tall and uncut instead.

That left the bald man, who was wounded but still dangerous. Fargo came up in a crouch, burst out from behind the rock, and ran across the road. No more shots sounded as he threw himself down into the grass. He lay there listening intently as his heart hammered in his chest.

He heard the sound of the river rushing over its rocky streambed. Earlier, birds had been singing in the trees, but they were all gone now, frightened off by the shots. Fargo listened harder.

A rustling in the grass, like a snake.

But it was too early in the season for snakes to be crawling.

Suddenly, with a furious shout, the bald man heaved up out of the grass and lunged toward Fargo. The gun in his hand roared as flame geysered from its barrel. Fargo rolled onto his back and felt the ground shiver under him as a bullet slammed into the dirt less than a foot away. The Colt bucked against his palm as he fired.

The bald man fell backward as if somebody had just slammed a tree trunk across his face. Fargo saw the pistol fly through the air as the man dropped it. With a lithe motion, the Trailsman uncoiled from the ground and stalked forward, keeping his revolver trained on the fallen man.

The front of the rough linsey-woolsey shirt under the man's black vest was stained with blood. The man coughed as he lay on his back, and more blood welled from his mouth. He looked up at Fargo with hate-filled eyes in which the life was fading fast.

"You . . . bastard," the dying man said gratingly. "Told Barker . . . not to . . . come after . . ."

He couldn't finish. His final breath rattled in his throat. The muscles in his arms and legs spasmed for a few seconds, and then he lay motionless in death.

Fargo looked up and down the river, checking for any signs of the other man, but no one was in sight. Barker, whoever he was, was gone.

Fargo's hat had fallen off when he leaped from the boulder. The cool breeze he had earlier enjoyed so much now riffled his thick black hair, but it wasn't the same.

No, sir, he thought, this beautiful day just wasn't anywhere near as nice anymore. Not after two men had tried to kill him and he didn't have the slightest idea why.

Fargo caught the dead man's horse, hefted the corpse over the saddle, and lashed it down. Then he fetched the Ovaro from the hiding place in the trees and resumed his journey to Fort Smith, leading the other mount with its grisly burden. Maybe somebody at Fort Smith would recognize the dead man.

As he rode, Fargo thought about the letter he had received from Grady Donaldson. Several years earlier, Grady had been the manager of a stage station on the Butterfield Line, over in New Mexico Territory. Fargo had ridden in there, having been shot up pretty bad after an encounter with some hostile Navajos; Grady had taken care of him, nursed him back to health. Skye Fargo wasn't the sort of man to forget something like that. He owed Grady Donaldson his life.

So when Grady's letter had caught up to him in St. Louis—asking that Fargo meet him in Fort Smith, Arkansas, between March 15 and April 15—Fargo had set out as soon as he could buy some supplies. The letter didn't say what Grady wanted, but only that it was urgent he see Fargo.

Whatever Grady wanted, Fargo would see it through if it were in his power to do so. He didn't think Grady was the sort to call in the favor Fargo owed him unless it really was important.

Fargo glanced back at the corpse. He didn't see how the attempt on his life could be tied in with Grady, but he had to admit that at this point, he just didn't know.

He would find out more when he got to Fort Smith. The Arkansas River made a big bend to the north and then curved back to the south. The road went straight on to the town, cutting cross-country for a couple of miles. Fort Smith was on that southward curve of the river, perched on a high bluff overlooking the spot where the smaller Poteau River flowed in from the southwest and merged with the larger stream. It was a bustling settlement, the largest town in this part of the country, and lights blazed in most of the buildings as Fargo rode in, not long after nightfall.

Grady's letter had said that he'd be staying at the Hamilton House. Fargo didn't recall the place from previous visits to Fort Smith, but he was sure he could find it. First, though, he had to deal with the dead body on the horse behind him.

Naturally enough, the corpse, strapped in the saddle and with its head down, drew some attention from passersby. Fargo hailed one of the curious men and asked where the sheriff's office was located these days. Receiving directions, he rode on down the street and drew rein in front of a squarish, redbrick building. A light burned in the window. Fargo swung down from the saddle, looped the reins of both horses around the hitch rail, and stepped up onto the low wooden porch in front of the office.

The man inside looked up from some papers on the desk in front of him as Fargo entered. He was in late middle age, with thinning white hair and a sweeping mustache. A badge glittered on the lapel of his coat. "Evenin', mister," he said to Fargo. "Something I can do for you?"

"You the sheriff?" Fargo asked.

"Yes, sir. Albin Brown's my name."

"Skye Fargo," the Trailsman responded. He jerked a thumb over his shoulder toward the street. "I've got a dead man out here."

That news brought a worried frown to Sheriff Albin Brown's face. "How'd he get dead?"

"I shot him," Fargo said bluntly. "He was trying to kill me at the time."

"Well, that's a mighty good reason to ventilate a fella." The lawman put his hands flat on the desk, shoved his chair back, and pushed himself to his feet. "Assumin', that is, that you're tellin' the truth. Let's have a look at this corpse."

Fargo didn't take offense at the sheriff's comment. It was a lawman's job not to take any statement at face value. Brown would have to investigate and then decide for himself on the truth of the matter. Fargo was willing to go along with that as long as the sheriff wasn't unreasonable about it.

Brown didn't put his hat on as he followed Fargo out of the office, but he did pick up a shotgun from where it hung on a couple of hooks attached to the wall. Fargo stepped off the porch and went to the side of the dead man's horse. He stooped for a second, pulled the Arkansas Toothpick from the sheath strapped to his leg, and used the long, heavy blade to cut the lashings that held the bald man in the saddle. The corpse started to slide. Fargo caught hold of the man's shirt and lowered him to the ground, face up.

Light from the sheriff's office spilled through the open door and illuminated the dead man's features. As people gathered around, Sheriff Brown studied the corpse and then grunted. "Never saw him before; at least not that I recollect." He looked around at the small group of townspeople and asked, "Anybody here know this feller?"

The townspeople shook their heads, and a couple of men spoke up in the negative. Fargo watched them carefully without appearing to, and he thought they were all telling the truth. The dead man was indeed a stranger here in Fort Smith.

The sheriff went on, "Hard to tell, once a feller's dead, but from the looks of him, he was a tough hombre. Tried to hold you up, did he?"

"I don't know what he was after," Fargo replied honestly. "He was following me, and when I confronted him, he went for his gun. There was another man with him, hanging back a ways, and he took a shot at me, too, before he lit a shuck out of there."

Sheriff Brown grunted again. "Bushwhackers. There are too many no-accounts like that around here. They were after your money and your goods, more than likely."

That was certainly a feasible explanation for the affair, Fargo thought, and yet some instinct inside him still wasn't convinced that that was all there was to it. He didn't mention anything about Grady Donaldson to the sheriff. As far as he knew, Grady's honesty was above reproach, but even so, Grady might not want the law getting mixed up in his business. Fargo wanted to find out what it was about first, before he said anything to Brown.

"You're satisfied with my explanation, then?" he asked.

"Why wouldn't I be?" Brown tucked the scattergun under his arm, no longer holding it ready in case he had to use it. "Folks get held up from time to time on the road, and they got a right to defend themselves. Unless somebody comes along to dispute it, I'll take your word for what happened, Fargo. Best not leave town right away, though, until we hold the inquest and get an official verdict from a coroner's jury."

"When will that be?"

"First thing in the morning."

Fargo nodded. That shouldn't be a problem, he thought. It was unlikely that Grady's business was so urgent that he would have to leave right away. After all, there was still over a week remaining in the time period Grady had mentioned in his letter.

With a gesture toward the corpse, Fargo went on, "You'll take care of this?"

"Sure. I'll walk down and fetch Abe Hooper. He's the undertaker around here, as well as bein' a good cabinetmaker and a passable barber and tooth-yanker."

Fargo unhitched the Ovaro. "I'll be around if you need me, Sheriff."

Brown nodded and gave him a casual wave as Fargo walked off, leading the stallion.

Several of the bystanders badgered him with questions. Fargo was polite but didn't tell them any more than he had told the sheriff. One of the townspeople provided directions to the Hamilton House.

It was a decent-looking hotel, constructed of thick, whitewashed planks, nothing fancy, but not squalid, either. Fargo tied the Ovaro outside and went into the lobby, planning to ask at the desk for Grady Donaldson.

He didn't have to do that. He was halfway across the lobby when he heard his name called.

He looked over to see Grady Donaldson stand up from an armchair and come toward him. Grady was in his forties, a stockily built man who was a little under medium height, with dark, graying hair and a mustache. He grabbed Fargo's hand and pumped it enthusiastically.

"Skye! Skye Fargo! Damn, but it's good to see you, you old hoss thief!"

Fargo grinned. "Take it easy with that horse-thief talk," he said as he returned Grady's handshake. "The law around here is already a mite suspicious of me."

"Oh? Why's that?"

"Because I brought a dead man into town with me."

Grady's eyes widened with a look of surprise. "What the hell!"

"I'll tell you all about it," Fargo said. "First, though,

10

I need to tend to my horse, and then maybe we can find a place to get a drink.''

"Sure. You still riding that big Ovaro?''

"Yep.''

"That's just about the finest horse I ever did see— and I've seen a lot of horses in my time. The hotel has a stable out back. You can put him there, once you check in.''

Grady just assumed Fargo was going to stay here, but that made sense, so Fargo didn't argue. He checked in with the slick-haired clerk at the desk, signing his name in the book but leaving blank the space for his home address. It had been a mighty long time since he'd had a permanent one of those. He liked to think the whole West was his home.

When the stallion was settled into a stall in the hotel stable, with plenty of water and grain, Fargo accompanied his friend upstairs to Grady's room. "I've got a bottle of whiskey in my warbag that's better than anything you'll find in the taverns around here,'' Grady promised.

He poured drinks for them and sat on the bed while Fargo sank into the room's single armchair. An oil lamp sputtered and hissed on a small table.

Grady lifted his glass and said, "To old friends and good times.''

"I'll drink to that,'' Fargo said, "although it wasn't really good times that brought us together.''

Grady tossed back the whiskey and then chuckled. "No, I reckon it wasn't. You'd lost more blood than any man has a right to and still be alive. I didn't know if you'd pull through or not.''

"I probably wouldn't have if not for you.''

"I don't know about that,'' Grady said with a shake of his head. "I never saw a fella with more scars than you, Skye. The Good Book says man is born to trouble, and you're living proof of that scripture if I ever saw it.''

Fargo sipped his whiskey. It was as good as Grady had promised.

"Now," Grady said, "tell me about this dead man you brought in."

Fargo was more interested in why Grady had summoned him here to Fort Smith, but he was willing to postpone his own questions for a few minutes. Quickly, he sketched the details of the violent encounter he'd had earlier in the day on the river road. He described the dead man and asked, "Sound like anybody you know?"

Grady frowned as he thought for a moment and then shook his head. "Nope, can't say as it does. I'd have to take a look at him to be sure, of course, but I don't think I know him."

"His partner is named Barker. That ring any bells?"

Again Grady considered the question, and again he shook his head. "I think there were some Barkers who lived not far from us when I was a kid, back in Kentucky. Haven't known any since then, though. Why do you ask, Skye? You don't think those two bush-whackers had anything to do with me, do you?"

"I didn't know," Fargo said with a shrug of his shoulders. "I don't know why you asked me to meet you here, Grady."

A solemn expression came over Grady's face. He had been enthused about seeing Fargo again and then curious about the corpse Fargo had brought into town, but as the Trailsman saw the shadows appear in Grady's eyes, he knew that his friend was a very worried man. Grady took a deep breath and seemed to age a little before Fargo's eyes.

"I need your help, Skye," he said.

Fargo nodded. "I figured as much. Anything I can do, I will. You know that."

"Yeah." Grady rubbed a hand wearily over his face. "I have a son—did you know that?"

"No. I don't recall anybody else being at that stage station over in New Mexico except a couple of hostlers."

"That's because the boy and his ma weren't there.

Ellen—my wife—she couldn't stand the frontier. She went back east to live and took Davey with her."

"That's rough," Fargo said. "You ever hear from them?"

"Oh, sure." Grady waved a hand. "Ellen never hated me; she just didn't want to live out in the middle of nowhere at some stage station. Can't say as I blamed her too much for that. She wrote to me now and then, and let the boy write to me, too."

"Where are they now?" Fargo asked.

Grady's fingers closed more tightly on the empty glass in his hand as he looked down at the floor. "Ellen passed on last year."

"I'm sorry to hear that," Fargo said.

"She never did divorce me, so I reckon I'm a widower now. I figured the boy—Dave—would stay back east, but he came west instead after his ma died."

"Came to the stage station, you mean?"

Grady shook his head. "I'm not running the place anymore. Old John Butterfield promoted me. I'm superintendent of the whole stretch from El Paso to Tucson."

"Congratulations," Fargo said with a smile. "I reckon you deserve it."

Grady scratched at an ear and shook his head. "Thanks. I do my best. Better at working for a stage line than being a father, I guess. Dave wouldn't come all the way to El Paso to see me. He had me meet him here in Fort Smith. When we got together . . . well, we didn't get along all that well."

"That's not too surprising," Fargo said. "You two don't really know each other if you've been apart for a long time. You just have to get used to each other."

"Yeah, that's what I told myself. I had to get back to work, but we made plans to meet again. But when I got here, Dave was gone."

"Gone?" Fargo said with a frown. "Gone where?"

Grady inclined his head toward the west. "Across the river into Indian Territory. He's been gone for months, Skye, and nobody's seen hide nor hair of him. I . . . I'm afraid something must have happened to him."

"What do you want me to do?" Fargo asked, even though he was pretty sure he already knew the answer to that question.

"I want you to find him, Skye," Grady said, and there was raw, naked fear on his face as he spoke. "I want you to find my boy and bring him back to me."

2

Fargo frowned at his whiskey for a long moment after Grady's fervent plea. He thought he understood what his friend felt, but he had no children of his own and couldn't be certain that he grasped the emotions going through Grady at this moment.

Despite his sympathy, Fargo had some reservations. He asked, "How old is Dave, Grady?"

"Why, he's . . ." Grady looked up at the ceiling for a second as he did the calculations in his head. "He's twenty-two, I reckon."

"Then he's a full-grown man. Seems to me his comings and goings are really his own business."

Grady's face darkened. "I'm his father, dammit! I got a right to know where he is and whether or not he's all right."

"Maybe," Fargo allowed. "But if I find him and bring him back here, and he doesn't want to come, that's pretty much the same as kidnapping."

Grady grabbed the bottle and splashed some more whiskey into his glass. "Sounds to me like you didn't mean it when you said you'd do anything you could to help me, Skye." He knocked back the fiery liquor in a single gulp.

Now Fargo was a little angry. It seemed to him that Grady was trying to take advantage of the situation.

"I make a habit of saying what I mean and meaning what I say. I'll find Dave for you, if he can be found.

And I'll bring him back if that's what he wants. But I'm not going to hogtie him and drag him back against his will."

Grady scowled at him for a moment and then dropped his gaze and rubbed his hand over his face again. "Lord, I'm sorry, Skye," he muttered. "I'm just out of my head, I reckon. I call Dave a boy, but I know he's a man. I don't want you to kidnap him. It's just that . . . we were apart for so long. Now . . . I want to make things right."

"Sure, I know you do," Fargo said easily as his own anger dissipated. "Tell me more about Dave."

"Like what?"

"You said he rode over into Indian Territory. Why? What business did he have over there?"

Grady shook his head. "I'm not sure. He said something about maybe going partners with some fellas in a freighting outfit that would run from here over to Tahlequah. But I don't know if that deal ever came about."

"He must have had friends here, then, if he talked about going into business with someone," Fargo pointed out. "I reckon you've already spoken to all of them?"

"Yeah, everybody I could find, but nobody who knew him very well. And none of them knew anything about a freight line."

Fargo frowned in thought and idly ran his thumbnail along his strong jawline, with its closely cropped black beard. He asked, "Can you make me a list of the people you talked to?"

"Well, sure, I guess," Grady said. "But what's the point?"

"I want to ask them some questions of my own."

"I already asked them to tell me everything they know about Dave. I don't see what they could tell you that'd be different."

"Maybe nothing," Fargo said, "but sometimes a fresh pair of ears hears things that somebody else didn't."

Grady shrugged. "I ain't the one to tell you how to go about your business. You're the Trailsman, after all. If anybody can find Dave, it's you."

Fargo played a hunch then and said quietly, "Grady, why don't you tell me what you're really thinking? You're worried that something has happened to your son—is that it?"

Grady stood up and began to pace back and forth, unable to sit still any longer. Fargo heard the ragged edge of nervous strain in his friend's voice as Grady said, "The thing of it is, I just don't know Dave all that well. I don't know what he's liable to have done. He doesn't know much about frontier ways. He could have agreed to go off into Indian Territory with those men, and they could have robbed him and killed him. There might not have ever been any freight line."

Fargo nodded slowly. "That's true," he said bluntly, not pulling any punches now. It was time he and Grady put all their cards on the table. He said, "Indian Territory can be a pretty lawless place. I may find that your son is dead."

Grady stopped pacing. He turned to face Fargo and drew a deep breath as he did so. "If that's what happened, I want to know it. The truth may hurt, but it's better than never knowing."

Fargo gave his friend a grim smile and nodded again. "I reckon you're right about that." He came to his feet. "Write up that list for me, and I'll pick it up in the morning, before I go to the inquest for that gent I had to kill."

"You'll get started right away, then?" Grady asked eagerly.

"No point in waiting," Fargo said. "The trail's just going to get colder."

The inquest, held at the county courthouse, was a simple affair, as Sheriff Albin Brown had predicted. Abraham Hooper, who, as it turned out, was the county judge and local coroner, as well as the undertaker, cabinetmaker, barber, and dentist, swore in a jury and directed Fargo to tell the jurors what had happened beside the Arkansas River the day before.

Fargo did so, and with no one on hand to contradict his testimony, the jury quickly ruled that the deceased—identity still unknown—had met his death at the hands of one Skye Fargo, who had acted legally and justifiably in self-defense. The dead man hadn't had anything in his pockets that might identify him, but he had been in possession of a ten-dollar gold piece, which would go to pay for the expenses for his burial. Hooper banged his gavel down and declared that the inquest was adjourned.

Grady Donaldson was the only spectator there. He stood up and came over to Fargo. Earlier, over breakfast in the hotel dining room, Grady had given Fargo the list he'd requested. Now, Grady said, "I'm ready to get started talking to these people if you are."

Fargo shook his head. "Just me, Grady, not you."

"But I figured I'd go with you," Grady protested.

"It'll be better if I talk to them by myself."

"Why?" Grady asked with a frown.

"It's possible some of those folks don't know that you and I are friends. When I start asking questions about Dave, they might be more likely to give me honest answers if you're not there."

"What are you saying? That Dave doesn't *want* me to find him?"

"That's a possibility, too, just like the possibility that he might be dead. You know the old saying—hope for the best but prepare for the worst."

"Yeah, I reckon," Grady grumbled. "What you say makes sense, Skye. But you can't blame me for wanting to be right there with you while you're looking for him."

"That's another thing," Fargo said. "When I ride over into Indian Territory, I'm going alone. You're not riding with me."

"What?" This time Grady looked and sounded

downright angry. "You won't let me go along to look for my own son?"

"I may have to move pretty fast. No offense, Grady, but you'd slow me down. And it can be dangerous over there, too—"

"You reckon I can't take care of myself?" Grady demanded hotly. "I ran that stage station for a long time, surrounded by hostile Navajo and Apache, bandidos from below the border, and white outlaws. I may not have gotten around as much as you, Skye, but I've seen my share of ruckuses!"

Fargo kept his response calm and reasonable. "I know that. You'll do to ride the river with, Grady. But again, I may have better luck finding Dave if you're not with me. And that El Paso to Tucson stretch of the Butterfield Line isn't going to run itself."

"Well, I reckon that's true," Grady admitted grudgingly. "The sooner I get back, the better, as far as the stage line's concerned. But dammit, Skye, I figured we'd do this together."

"It's better this way," Fargo insisted. "Trust me."

"If I didn't, I never would've sent for you. Wouldn't have wasted your time or mine." Grady sighed. "All right, if that's the way it's got to be. But if you find out anything before you leave town, you'll tell me, won't you?"

"Sure," Fargo promised. "For now, why don't you go back to the hotel and try to relax?"

"Easier said than done, my friend, easier said than done."

Fargo smiled and clapped his friend on the shoulder. "I have confidence in you, Grady."

With that, Fargo left the courthouse. Grady had written down not only the names of people in Fort Smith who had been acquainted with his son Dave, but also where Fargo could find them. Fargo headed first for the local blacksmith shop. According to Grady's list, Dave had been friends with the smith, a man named Dumont.

Fargo spent the morning going from place to place

in the settlement, talking to people who had known Dave Donaldson. The young man had lived for seven or eight months in Fort Smith and had worked at several jobs during that time. From what Fargo could glean, Dave had been well liked and had done well at his jobs, which included: hostler at a livery stable, clerk at a land office, and assistant to a surveyor. He hadn't been fired from any of the jobs; instead, he had quit each of them, citing a restless nature that made him want to move on and do something else. He had remained friendly with the people he had worked for.

While he talked to the townspeople, Fargo passed himself off as an old friend of Dave's who had heard that he lived here in Fort Smith. Everyone seemed to accept the story without hesitation. Unfortunately, none of them had any idea where Dave was now—at least, not that they would admit. Nor did they know anything about Dave joining forces with some other men to start a freight line that would run into Indian Territory. Fargo's instincts told him that they were telling the truth.

The last name on his list was that of Matt Kenton. When Fargo asked the surveyor if he happened to know Kenton, the man frowned and said, "I'm sorry to say that I do."

"What do you mean by that?" Fargo asked.

"Kenton is the one fella those of us who knew Dave wished that he wouldn't associate with. Kenton's a gambler. Used to work the riverboats over on the Mississippi, but now he stays mostly around here. You can find him dealing poker over at the Ozark Palace Saloon, but not until tonight. Kenton's the sort who doesn't wake up until the sun's going down." The disapproval was easy to hear in the surveyor's voice.

Fargo nodded. "Much obliged."

"Say, do you know Grady Donaldson?" the man asked suddenly.

"Any relation to Dave?" Fargo asked, his tone seeming innocent and only casually interested.

"His pa. He came around not long ago looking for

Dave, too. I think he's still in town. You might look him up and see if he's heard anything about where Dave might be."

Fargo nodded. "Again, I'm obliged. I'll do that."

He left the surveyor's office. He had drawn a blank so far, but he wasn't really surprised. He hadn't really expected to turn up any information that Grady had missed, though anything was possible. And he still had Matt Kenton to talk to.

Fargo went back to the hotel, ate lunch in the dining room, and sprawled out on the bed in his room for a nap. He didn't get into town all that often, so he liked to take advantage of a real bed while he had one. Of course, any bed was better with a good-looking woman in it, he thought as he dozed off, but a fella couldn't have everything.

He woke up at dusk, as refreshed as always, whether he slept twenty minutes or twelve hours. After washing his face with water from the basin in the room, he went downstairs. He didn't see Grady anywhere, which was all right. He didn't have any news to report, and now that he had launched his investigation into Dave Donaldson's disappearance, it was better that as few people as possible saw him and Grady together.

The Ozark Palace Saloon wasn't very palatial. It was on a side street not far from the hotel, a tall, narrow stone building perched on a hillside. Fargo opened the thick wooden door and went in.

The barroom was dimly lit. Thick clouds of tobacco smoke clogged the air. A polished hardwood bar ran along the right side of the narrow, high-ceilinged room. Booths were on the other wall, with tables in between. Fargo saw a poker game going on at one of the rear tables and wondered if the dealer was Matt Kenton.

Fargo first strolled over to the bar and ordered a beer from a sleeve-gartered bartender. The beer wasn't very cold, but other than that, it tasted all right. Fargo inclined his head toward the poker table and asked the bartender, "That an open game?"

"Sure, if you've got the stakes," the bartender replied. "Kenton doesn't play penny ante."

Fargo nodded, grateful that his hunch had paid off. He wasn't hurting for money at the moment. He could afford to invest a little in the game, in return for a chance to talk to Matt Kenton.

Before he could do that, however, a hand laid a soft touch on his arm, and he turned to see a young woman smiling up at him.

She was short and lushly curved, with light brown hair that fell around her face and shone even in the saloon's dim light. The low-cut gown she wore revealed the upper halves of her large, creamy breasts. Her eyes were a startling blue.

"Buy a girl a drink, mister?" she asked with a smile.

Over the years, Fargo had heard that question a hundred times from a hundred different saloon girls. Something about this one was truly different, though. Her smile looked genuine, not practiced or artificial. Either she was relatively new at this game, or she was very, very good at it.

He felt himself harden a little as her hand stroked his arm. Under other circumstances, he would have been glad to spend the evening with her and maybe even take her to bed, but right now he had more pressing concerns.

"I'm sorry, darlin'," he said with a smile. "I have a previous engagement with some cards. Maybe another time."

Her full lips started to make a disappointed pout, but then she abruptly gave it up and grinned at him. "You're sure?" she asked.

"I'm afraid so."

"Well, another time, then."

Fargo nodded. "Sure."

She moved her hand up his arm and to the back of his neck, and came up on her toes as she pulled his head down. "Just so you won't forget . . . ," she said, and then she kissed him.

22

Her lips were warm and sweet and hungry, and her kiss was full of honest passion. Her tongue met Fargo's with a bold, wet caress. His manhood hardened even more as she molded her ripe young body against his. When she finally pulled away from him, she still wore her friendly grin.

"There," she said in satisfaction.

Fargo chuckled. "Don't worry, ma'am. I won't forget you."

"I didn't think you would." With that, she sashayed away. Instead of approaching one of the other men at the bar, she went to an empty table and sat down alone, where she continued to smile at Fargo.

Fargo turned back to the bar to finish his beer. The bartender drifted over and said, "I see Lydia's taken a shine to you."

"Lydia? She didn't tell me her name." Fargo swallowed the last of the beer and put the empty mug on the bar. "I reckon she'll find somebody else to console herself with."

The bartender shook his head. "Nope. That ain't the way it works. Once Lydia sets her sights on a fella, he's the only one she's interested in. Guess you could say, because of that, she's not really cut out for her line of work."

"I reckon not," Fargo murmured. He pushed the mug across the bar. "Refill that, and then I'll go see about that poker game."

"Sure. But when you get done playing cards, Lydia will be waiting for you."

Fargo glanced at the young woman again. The prospect of having her waiting for him was an appealing one.

He carried the beer over to the table where Matt Kenton dealt poker hands. The size of the pot in the middle of the table told Fargo that the bartender had been right about this not being a penny-ante game.

Matt Kenton was in his thirties and clean-shaven, with closely cropped sandy hair and a blunt chin. He wore a suit that was good but not flashy, and had a black hat thumbed to the back of his head. His face was utterly expressionless as he studied his cards.

"Raise forty," Kenton said as he shoved a couple of gold pieces into the pile.

The next man shook his head and tossed in his hand. "Too damn rich for me," he said. "In fact, that cleans me out."

"Be sorry to see you go," Kenton said tonelessly.

"Well, I'm not going anywhere," said the next man around the table. "I'll see you and raise you twenty." Coins clinked as he tossed them into the pot.

The other two men in the game folded as well, leaving just Kenton and the man who had raised his bet in the game. Kenton glanced at his cards for a second, and then he said, "I'll call." He pushed more money into the pile and placed his cards faceup on the table. "Royal flush."

"Son of a—" The other man stared across the table at Kenton. "How the hell did you do that?" he said. His own hand, which he dropped on the table, showed a full house, jacks over tens.

Kenton smiled thinly and began to rake in the pot. He responded, "Just lucky, I guess."

"Lucky, hell!"

Kenton froze as a sudden air of tension gripped the other men around the table. As Kenton took his eyes off the pot to stare across at his vanquished opponent, the rest of the players began to edge back. Fargo knew what they were thinking: gunplay was liable to break out at any second. He was ready to get out of the line of fire, too. He hoped that Kenton wouldn't wind up dead before he had the chance to ask the gambler some questions.

Quietly, Kenton asked, "Just what do you mean by that, friend?"

The other man swallowed hard. "I . . . I know that sounded bad, Matt. I didn't mean it like that, honest. I just meant that luck didn't have anything to do with it. That was good, honest poker playing. That's all—I swear."

Kenton moved again, pulling in the pot. The other men relaxed. Kenton said simply, "Oh."

The other man babbled, "You know I'd never—"

Kenton's cool voice cut him off. "Another hand, gentlemen?"

"Not for me," said the player who'd already said he was cleaned out. He pushed back his chair and stood up.

Fargo rested his hand on the back of the empty chair. "I'll sit in, if that's all right with everybody."

Kenton gathered up the cards and began to shuffle them. "As long as you've got money, friend, it's all right with me." The other players nodded, including the one who had nearly given Kenton a mortal insult. That man pulled a handkerchief from his pocket and mopped sweat from his pale face.

Fargo took a leather poke from his pocket and placed it on the table in front of him. He undid the drawstring, and spilled coins from the poke.

"Five-dollar ante," Kenton said. Fargo tossed a gold piece into the center of the table as the other men anted up.

The first hand he drew was good enough to stay in for a couple of rounds of bets, but not good enough to win. The second one netted him a small pot and the deal, which he gave back to Kenton on the third hand. Fargo had played a lot of poker over the years. He was a good player, not overly cautious but not the sort to plunge wildly, either, and he truly enjoyed the game. Several more hands went by, and an hour had passed before he knew it.

He figured that was long enough to wait. He was ready to say something about Dave Donaldson. Before he did, though, he glanced toward the table where Lydia had been sitting earlier.

She was still there, he saw, and as their eyes met for a moment across the smoky room, she smiled.

Fargo returned the smile, but he had mixed emotions about it. Lydia was beautiful, and he had responded strongly when she kissed him. On the other hand, right now, he really didn't need the distraction of this lovely, lusty young woman. He had to concentrate on the job he was doing for Grady Donaldson.

He turned his attention back to the poker game. He threw away a couple of cards, but the ones he drew to replace them didn't improve his hand. Still, he stayed in the game for the time being.

"Any of you boys happen to know a fella named Donaldson?" he asked in an idly curious voice. In some games, the players talked a lot, but not in this one. There had been some conversation, though, so Fargo didn't think it would seem unusual for him to ask a question or two.

"Friend of yours?" said one of the other men, not Matt Kenton.

"That's right," Fargo said. "I heard he was here in Fort Smith; thought I'd look him up and say howdy."

"Would this be Dave Donaldson?" Kenton asked. As always, it was hard to tell much from his tone of voice.

"That's right. You know him?"

"Sure," Kenton said with a shrug. "He used to come in here and play some cards, have a drink every now and then."

"I remember him, too," one of the other players said. "Haven't seen him in a while, though."

Kenton nodded. "That's what I was about to say. It's been at least a couple of months since he was here last."

"You think he moved on?" Fargo asked.

"Don't have any thoughts on the matter, one way or the other," the gambler replied. He pushed a coin into the center of the table. "Raise ten."

Fargo let it go and saw the raise. It appeared that Matt Kenton's friendship with Dave Donaldson had, at best, been casual. Of course, it was possible that

Kenton was concealing something, but Fargo had no reason to think that was the case. He had to walk a fine line between asking questions and being too suspicious.

He continued playing for another half hour, not wanting it to appear that he was overly interested in Dave Donaldson's whereabouts. When he pushed back his chair and called it a night, he was down only twelve dollars—which he thought was pretty good, considering Kenton's skill with the pasteboards.

Kenton gave him a thin smile, the first real expression Fargo had seen on the man's face. "Enjoyed the game. Come back anytime."

"Thanks. So did I."

Fargo turned away from the poker table and looked across the room toward the table where Lydia had been sitting earlier. To his surprise, she wasn't there. He hadn't noticed her leaving the saloon, but when he looked around, he didn't see her anywhere.

Oh, well, Fargo thought. He tried not to feel disappointed. He had stayed in the game for quite a while. He couldn't blame Lydia for getting tired of waiting for him.

He left the Ozark Palace Saloon, walked around the corner and back down the street toward the Hamilton House. He decided that when he reached the hotel, he wouldn't talk to Grady Donaldson just yet. He hadn't found out a thing in Fort Smith, so it looked like he would have to continue his search for Dave in Indian Territory. He could ride over to Tahlequah—the settlement that was the capital of the Cherokee Nation—and find out if a new freight line had gone into operation there. If the line existed, its headquarters sure wasn't here in Fort Smith.

He would talk to Grady before he rode out in the morning, Fargo decided as he climbed the stairs to the hotel's second floor. He needed to find out how to get word to his friend, once he'd found out something about Dave. Assuming, of course, that the young man wasn't lying in a shallow grave somewhere in Indian Territory, never to be found.

Fargo had lived a dangerous life, and it had instilled certain habits in him. One of those habits was to mark his door when he stayed in a hotel, so that he could tell if anyone had been in his room. The hair he had left between the door and the jamb was now gone, he saw by the light of the lamp at the end of the hall. His hand went to the butt of his holstered Colt as his muscles tensed.

His other hand tried the knob. It was locked, the way he had left it. He was convinced, though, that someone had entered his room. And might, in fact, still be in there. He took the key from the pocket of his buckskin shirt and slipped it slowly and quietly into the lock.

The lock made such a little sound, as Fargo turned the key, that he hoped anyone inside the room wouldn't notice. He dropped the key back into his pocket, grasped the doorknob, and drew his revolver. With a sudden twist of the knob, he threw the door open and rushed into the room, dropping into a crouch as he swept the Colt's barrel from one side to the other.

A startled gasp came from the bed. "Oh, my Lord!" a female voice exclaimed.

Light from the hall spilled into the room. Fargo straightened and frowned as he looked at the bed. The young woman called Lydia lay there under the covers, with the sheet pulled up to her chin.

Fargo was willing to bet that under that sheet she didn't have on a stitch of clothing.

3

Fargo relaxed slightly but didn't lower the Colt just yet. More than once in his life, some hombre who wanted to kill him had tried to use a pretty girl as a distraction.

"Mister, what are you doing?" Lydia asked. "I promise you, you don't need that gun."

Fargo heeled the door shut behind him. A lamp burned on the little table beside the bed, its wick turned low.

"How did you get in?" he asked her.

She shrugged, which caused the sheet to slip down a little on her shoulders. They were bare and quite attractive. "Locks don't mean much to me. I've always been good with them."

"So you're a thief," Fargo said.

"I am not!" Lydia sounded offended. She raised herself on her elbow and made the sheet slip even more. "I just wanted to talk to you. If I was a thief, would I have waited for you?"

"A better question is, What are you doing in my bed?" Fargo pointed out. "If you just wanted to talk to me, you could have waited downstairs in the lobby. Or you could have stayed at the Ozark Palace."

She waved a hand. A dark nipple—the size of a silver dollar—peeked out from under the edge of the sheet. She said, "That place is full of smoke and other smells. It's more pleasant here. And as for what I'm doing in your bed . . . well, isn't it obvious?"

"Maybe so, but that involves more than talking."

"Oh!" she exclaimed in frustration. She sat up and removed the sheet. That gave him a good look at her bare breasts as they bounced a little from the motion. They were creamy globes of female flesh, large but fairly firm, crowned with erect nipples that plainly stood out. "You are the most maddening man! Do you have to take everything I say so literally?"

Fargo had looked around the room and checked the window, and he was now convinced that no bushwhackers lurked anywhere in the immediate vicinity. "Folks should say what they mean," he told her.

She rolled her eyes and muttered, "Lord have mercy." She threw the sheet back and revealed the rest of her nude body. "Are we going to do this or not? Is that plainspoken enough for you?"

Fargo finally holstered his Colt as he chuckled. "I reckon so." He hung his hat on the back of the single chair and peeled his shirt over his head. Then he paused and added, "Don't you think it might be a good idea if we knew each other's name first?" Of course, he already knew her name, but he didn't tell her that.

She swung her legs off the bed and stood up to come toward him. Her breasts did that intriguing bobble again. "We can save that for later," she said. "Right now I just want you out of those buckskins."

Lydia helped Fargo take off the rest of his clothes, and as she did, he got a good look at the rest of her body. She had plenty of curves, from lush thighs to rounded hips to those impressive breasts. The triangle of hair between her legs was thick and a slightly darker shade of brown than the hair on her head. He put her age at nineteen or twenty, but the way she purred in anticipation, as she wrapped her fingers around his stiff manhood, told him she was no blushing innocent.

She kept hold of him and led him to the bed in that way. She lay down and spread her legs. Evidently, she expected him to climb on and get started right away.

Instead, Fargo lowered himself to the mattress beside her. He cupped her left breast in his hand and used his thumb to stroke the pebbled nipple. Lydia caught her breath, as if she were both excited and surprised by the gentle caress.

Fargo brought his head down to her breast and sucked her nipple into his mouth. As his lips closed around the hard bud of flesh and his tongue began to lave it, Lydia said, "Oh, my . . . oh, my . . . yes . . . please don't stop . . ."

After a few moments, Fargo paused, but only to transfer his mouth to her other nipple. Lydia ran her fingers through his dark hair and clutched his head to her breast. Fargo slid his hand down over the gently rounded curve of her belly and rested it on the soft fur that covered the mound between her legs. Lydia said, "Ahhh. . . . ," as he pressed down lightly on it.

He let his middle finger slide lower still and found the slick opening at her core. His finger delved into her and explored the hot, wet center of her femininity. In an involuntary response to this penetration, her hips bounced up off the bed as she gave a throaty, breathless cry of passion.

Fargo's shaft was as hard as a bar of iron, and it throbbed with the need to plunge into her depths. But his will was like iron, too, and he controlled himself with relative ease. He wanted to give her as much pleasure as he could before he slaked his own desires.

Lydia's head tossed back and forth on the pillow as she writhed under his arousing touch. She clutched at his shoulders and pumped her hips as he added a second finger to the first one. Suddenly, she stiffened, and then a shudder went through her as her climax gripped her. Slowly, she sank back on the bed, wound her arms around Fargo's neck, and pulled his face to hers. Their mouths met.

This kiss was even fiercer and hungrier than the one in the Ozark Palace Saloon. Their tongues dueled sensuously as Fargo moved over her and poised himself between her thighs. He teased her with the head of his organ. Her flesh seemed searingly hot to the sensitive skin that sheathed his manhood. Fargo began to ease his shaft into her.

Once again, Lydia's passion and impulsive nature got the better of her. She thrust with her hips and engulfed the long, thick pole of male flesh that jutted out proudly from Fargo's groin. He couldn't hold back any longer and met her thrust with one of his own that sheathed him completely inside her. After holding that position for a moment, his hips launched into the timeless, universal rhythm of a man and a woman giving each other pleasure.

Fargo's arousal built rapidly. He had already waited quite a while. Lydia's large, cushiony breasts flattened under him as he pinned her to the bed and drove into her at a faster, harder pace. She panted and breathlessly urged him on, saying, "Faster, Skye, faster! Oh, my God! Harder!"

Fargo rode her at a gallop and gave her everything he had to give. When his climax swept over him, he surrendered to it willingly and drove as deeply into her as he could. Lydia's arms around his neck held him more tightly than ever.

Though Fargo's culmination seemed endless, eventually it was over. Beneath him, Lydia gave a long sigh. Fargo closed his eyes, drew a deep breath, gathered what was left of his depleted strength, and rolled over, taking her with him. His member was still buried inside her.

He didn't stop rolling when he was on his back, however. Instead, he kept right on going until he reached the edge of the bed. Lydia fell off first, on the bottom. She said, "Oof!" as her ample rump hit the floor. Fargo had already let go of her. Agilely, he caught himself on hands and knees and straddled her.

His hand shot out toward the chair where he had placed his coiled gunbelt.

He snatched the Colt out of its well-oiled holster and lunged to his feet, pivoting to cover both the door and the window as he put his back against the wall. If anyone tried to break into the room, they would get a hot-lead welcome.

From the floor, Lydia sputtered, "Wha . . . what . . . what the *hell*!"

Fargo fixed her with a stony gaze. "Stay there," he snapped. For a few seconds during their lovemaking, passion and excitement had threatened to completely overwhelm his reasoning ability, but a part of his brain had remained alert and had been aware of the warning bells going off in the back of his mind. He asked Lydia, "Was there a signal you were supposed to give, maybe something you were supposed to yell out when it was time to ambush me?"

Apparently confused, she stared at him for a moment and finally said angrily, "What in blue blazes are you talking about?" She reached beneath her to rub her bottom. "I could have broken something!"

Fargo would have felt foolish standing there naked with a gun in his hand, if he hadn't known that she had lied to him. Since he couldn't trust her, he had to find out what her game was. However, it was beginning to look as if she hadn't intended to decoy him to his death. No would-be assassins had burst into the room.

"You called me by name," he said. "I asked you before we got down to business if you wanted us to introduce ourselves, and you said it could wait until later."

"Oh." Fargo could almost see the wheels of her brain revolve inside her head as she tried to come up with a reasonable explanation. "I . . . I guess I must have heard someone call you by name in the saloon and remembered without really thinking about it."

Fargo nodded but didn't lower the gun. "Well, that

makes sense. At least, it would if I had told anyone in the saloon my name." He paused. "I didn't."

"Well, then . . . you must have . . . I must . . . I guess. . . . Oh, hell!" She threw her hands in the air, and even under the circumstances, the gesture was appealing. "I give up. I know you're Skye Fargo, the one people call the Trailsman. Aren't you?"

"That's right," Fargo admitted. "Did somebody put you up to this? Were you supposed to keep me busy while something happened somewhere else?" He suddenly thought about Grady Donaldson, and worry shot through him.

"No, of course not. I'm not working with anybody else. This was my own idea."

"Why?" Fargo asked. "What do you want from me, if you're not out to rob me or set me up for an ambush?"

She looked up at him from the floor and said, "I want you to help me find Dave Donaldson."

Fargo couldn't help staring at her. "Donaldson?" he repeated. "What do you know about Dave Donaldson?"

"More than you," she said. "If you want to talk about it, why don't we get dressed first? This is a little awkward, sitting on the floor with no clothes on."

Fargo thought about it for a second and then nodded. "All right. You can get dressed. But don't try anything." He lowered the gun and placed it on the table, where he could snatch it up in the blink of an eye if necessary.

Lydia seemed to be waiting for something. After a moment she said, "Aren't you going to help me up?"

"I reckon you can get up by yourself." Fargo prided himself on being a gentleman, but in this case, he wanted to keep his distance until he was sure what this beautiful but odd young woman was up to.

"Oh, all right." She got to her feet, leaning a hand on the bed as she did so. When she was up, she looked defiantly at Fargo and said, "Well?"

"Well what?"

"Aren't you going to turn around while I get dressed? Or are you going to be an absolute boor about this?"

Considering the intimacies they had shared a few minutes earlier, Fargo thought it was a little silly that she wanted him to turn around. He also didn't want her to pull a dagger or a derringer from her clothes and try to kill him. "You can turn around if you want," he said.

She blew a strand of hair out of her face with a frustrated sigh and turned around to pull her clothes on. Fargo stepped into his trousers but left his boots and shirt off. He strapped the gunbelt around his waist, though, and slipped the Colt back in its holster.

"Now," he said to Lydia as she reached behind her to finish buttoning up her gown, "tell me what this is all about."

"I told you. I want you to help me find Dave Donaldson."

"How do you know Dave?"

"He's a friend of mine. I met him several months ago when he first came to Fort Smith. If you must know, Dave and I . . . well, we're more than friends, really."

Fargo nodded toward the rumpled bed. "Didn't stop you from romping with me."

"I didn't say we were betrothed, or anything like that. Maybe . . . maybe I wouldn't have minded, if he had ever asked me, but—" She stopped with an abrupt shake of her head. "Let's just leave it that Dave and I were good friends, and I want to know what happened to him."

"Who says anything happened to him?" Fargo asked.

"Well, he rode off into Indian Territory and never came back! Something must have happened."

"The way I understand it, he's only been gone a couple of months," Fargo pointed out. "That's not really very long."

Lydia sat down on the edge of the bed. "Before he left, he told me he would be back in less than a month. It doesn't take more than a couple of weeks to ride to Tahlequah and back."

"That's where he was going? Tahlequah?"

"That's right. You should know that. You've talked to his father."

"You know Grady, too?"

She shook her head. "Not really. I saw him in the saloon and heard him talking to Matt Kenton and some of the other men. I heard him mention Tahlequah, so I figured he knew about that freight line Dave talked about starting."

"Did you talk to Grady yourself?"

"No." Lydia smiled ruefully. "I thought about introducing myself to him, but then I decided that no father would be very happy to find out that his son was involved with a . . . a girl like me."

Fargo thought she wasn't giving herself quite enough credit, but this was neither the time nor the place for that discussion. Instead, he said, "That explains how you know about Grady Donaldson. Now, how do you know about my connection with him?"

She smiled. "I followed him back to his hotel and saw him writing a letter to somebody. I wanted to find out what it was about, because I thought it might have something to do with Dave. So when he went to mail it, I followed him again. The postmaster was willing to let me read the letter and then seal it back up."

Fargo grunted. "How'd you convince him to go along with that?"

"The postmaster has been married to the same woman for over twenty years." Lydia smiled. "How do you *think* I convinced him?"

Fargo waved that off. "Never mind. So you read the letter Grady wrote to me."

"Yes, and even though he didn't say anything about Dave in the letter, I knew that had to be the reason he sent for you. After all, you're the famous Trails-man. Why else would he want you to meet him here?"

"We've been friends for a long time."

"All the more reason to turn to you for help."

Fargo couldn't argue with her logic. Besides, what she had told him might well be the answer to another question that had been bothering him. "I reckon you must know a man named Barker," he said bluntly.

Her brow creased in a slight frown. "Barker?" she repeated. "No, I don't think so."

"You didn't warn Barker that I was on my way to Fort Smith?"

"No." Her tone was that of an adult explaining something to a particularly dense child. "I told you, I don't know anybody named Barker. Who is he?"

"He and another fella tried to bushwhack me out on the river road yesterday, between here and Darda-nelle," Fargo explained. "Barker got away. The other man didn't."

"Then why don't you ask him—?" Lydia did not finish the question, as the answer dawned on her: "Oh. You killed him."

Fargo shrugged. "Seemed like the thing to do at the time." He described the dead man. "Does he sound familiar to you? You know anybody who looks like that?"

"Not at all. I'm not saying that I've never seen him around the saloon. But I don't remember him—I'm sure of that."

Fargo didn't know whether to believe her or not. So far, her explanations sounded plausible, and he felt an instinctive liking for her. But beautiful women had lied to him more than once in his life. His natural caution told him to reserve judgment.

She must have seen the look of skepticism on his face. "Skye, I'm telling you the truth," she insisted. "In fact, I'll tell you anything you want to know. My name, for starters. It's Lydia. Lydia Mallory."

Fargo didn't mention that the bartender at the Ozark Palace Saloon had already told him her first name. He nodded and said, "Miss Mallory."

"There's no need to be so formal. Not after what we did a little while ago." She inclined her head toward the bed. "I'll call you Skye, and you'll call me Lydia. If you'd like, I'll tell you all about how I came to be working in that place, but it's not a very pretty story, or a very interesting one, for that matter."

Fargo shook his head. "That's not necessary. Your past is your business, not mine."

"Thank you." She came closer to him, close enough to reach out and touch his bare chest with the tips of her fingers. "And I won't ask you about your past, although by the looks of those scars, it's been an adventurous one."

Fargo enjoyed the feel of her hand on his chest, but he didn't allow it to distract him. He said, "Since you've read Grady's letter, there's no point in lying to you. I'm looking for Dave Donaldson, all right. That's why I was in the Ozark Palace tonight."

"Because Dave used to play cards there with Matt Kenton," she responded.

It was a statement, not a question, but Fargo said, "That's right. Kenton's name was on a list of Dave's friends and acquaintances that Grady gave me. I've been checking with all of them to see if they know anything else about Dave's disappearance."

"My name wasn't on that list, was it?"

"No, it wasn't."

If that omission bothered Lydia, she gave no sign of it. "I'm not surprised. Dave and I kept our friendship pretty quiet. He wouldn't have told his father about us. That's one more reason I never went to talk to Mr. Donaldson. I thought that's the way Dave would want it."

By now Fargo was almost willing to accept Lydia's story. His gut told him she was telling the truth, and he had learned to accept the judgments he made of a person's character. He smiled faintly and said, "You know, you didn't have to come to my room to get me to look for Dave. I'm already doing that."

"I know." She rested both hands on his muscular chest and leaned closer to him. "The real reason I waited for you up here, instead of down in the lobby, is that I find you a very attractive man."

She looked up at him, with her soft lips parted, and Fargo said to himself, "The hell with it," and kissed her again. She urgently pressed herself against his bare torso. He brought up his left hand and cupped her right breast, kneading the soft flesh. Her lips parted, and she moaned as his tongue slipped into her mouth.

"Oh, Skye," she murmured when he broke the kiss, "I'm so glad you're taking me to Indian Territory."

Fargo put both hands on her shoulders and moved her back a step. "What?" he said.

"I said, I'm glad you're taking me——"

"I'm not taking you with me," he said. He didn't allow her to finish. Why did everyone assume that they were going with him into Indian Territory? First it was Grady, and now this lovely young woman called Lydia.

"But . . . but I thought I'd help you find Dave." She looked and sounded upset. "I have to go with you."

"No, you don't," Fargo said. "I work best alone."

"But I know where he is!"

Fargo's hands tightened on her shoulders. He looked at her intently as he said, "How can that be? You just asked me to find him. Why do you need my help if you know where he is?"

"Well, I don't really *know* . . . Skye—you're hurting me."

Fargo let go of her shoulders. He supposed that his fingers had pressed down on her flesh harder than he had intended. "Sorry," he muttered. "But I still want to know what you're talking about."

She turned away and paced back and forth for a moment, before stopping to look at him again. "Several times while we were together, Dave mentioned a place in Indian Territory . . . just the name of it, really. I don't know where it is or if it's a town or something else. But I got the feeling it was important, and that it had something to do with that freight line."

"Tell me the name," Fargo said.

Lydia opened her mouth as if to speak but then remained silent as a defiant look came into her eyes. Fargo saw the look and knew that he was in for trouble.

She crossed her arms over her ample bosom and said, "I won't tell you unless you promise to take me with you."

"No deal," Fargo growled. "I'll find Dave without your help if I have to."

"But if you have a starting place, it'll be a lot easier, won't it?"

Fargo glowered at her, but she became impassive in the face of his anger. He wasn't the sort of man who could force information or anything else out of a woman. A part of him might want to grab her shoulders and shake the name out of her, but he would never do that.

"If you really care about Dave, you'll tell me," he pointed out. "The sooner I find him, the better."

"What if he's not in trouble at all?"

"Then he should have been back by now. You said that yourself."

Lydia's white teeth caught at her bottom lip for a second as Fargo's logic pointed out the flaw in her argument. But she said resolutely, "I don't care. You give me your word, or you'll just have to find Dave without my help."

"All right," Fargo said with a nod. "That's exactly what I'll do." He reached over and grasped the doorknob. "I reckon we're through."

It was a bluff, at least to a certain extent. He thought Lydia really wanted to tell him what she knew, but she was set on using the information to get her own way. Fargo thought she might crack if he acted as if it just didn't matter to him.

She glared at him for a long moment but then sighed and said in disgust, "Oh, all right! If you're going to be that way about it, I'll tell you. I have to do what's best for Dave."

Fargo nodded, and said gently, "Now you're thinking straight. What's the name of this place?"

"It's not a very nice name." Fargo thought Lydia might be stalling again, but then she took a deep breath and went on, "It's called Devil's Den."

4

Devil's Den. Lydia was right, Fargo thought—it wasn't a very appealing name. The chances were, the place it described wasn't very appealing, either.

Fargo had been to Indian Territory before, and he didn't recall a settlement by that name. More than likely, it belonged to some geographic feature. Much of Indian Territory was rolling prairie, but there was some rugged terrain over there, too, especially in the eastern third of the territory, which happened to be where the Cherokee Reservation and the town of Tahlequah were located.

More and more, it appeared likely that the answer to Dave Donaldson's disappearance would be found somewhere between Fort Smith and the Cherokee capital.

"Now that I've told you, don't you think it's fair that you let me come along?" Lydia asked.

Fargo grinned at her. "Nice try, but the answer is still the same. You're staying here in Fort Smith."

She put her hands on her hips and said hotly, "You can't tell me what to do! I don't have to stay here if I don't want to!"

"No, I reckon not," Fargo admitted. "You're a grown woman and can go wherever you want to. But I *can* tell you that you're not going with me."

Her chin came up. "Maybe I don't want to go with

you anymore. Maybe I'll go looking for Devil's Den by myself."

Fargo shook his head. "That would be a bad mistake. There's no law over in the Nations except for tribal law on some of the reservations. Outlaws from all over congregate there. You won't find a more dangerous stretch of ground in the whole country, now that the old Natchez Trace is cleaned up."

"I don't care—," she began, but then she stopped and sank down on the edge of the bed. "Oh, who am I trying to fool? We both know I won't go traipsing off into Indian Territory. I'm not completely mad."

"No, you're not," Fargo told her as he went over to her and put his hand on her shoulder. "You're just worried about Dave. But I promise you, Lydia, I'll get word to you as soon as I find out anything. I'm already going to be getting in touch with Grady, so I might as well send a message to you, too."

She looked up at him. "You're not taking Mr. Donaldson with you?"

"Nope. So you see, it's not just you. Like I said, I work better alone."

She patted his hand where it rested on her shoulder. "All right, Skye. I believe you. Thank you for being patient with me."

"I reckon I owe you that much," Fargo said.

"You don't owe me anything. I'm just glad you don't think I'm plotting against you anymore." She stood up and touched her rump gingerly. "Although, I haven't totally forgiven you for dumping me on the floor that way."

Fargo couldn't restrain the laugh that welled up from inside him. "Sorry," he said.

"Oh, I don't blame you, once you've explained everything. I just haven't forgiven you."

She moved closer to him, and he followed his instincts and put his arms around her. She snuggled against his chest. She was short enough so that he had to lean over to inhale the clean fragrance of her thick brown hair.

"Bring Dave back safely if you can," she whispered, "but you come back safe, too, Skye."

He put his finger under her chin and tilted her head up and back so that he could kiss her again. "I'll try," he said as his lips brushed hers.

But that was the only promise he would make. With the life he led, there were no guarantees . . . except that sooner or later, trouble would explode all over again.

Lydia probably would have spent the night there, but Fargo eased her out of his room. He planned to get an early start in the morning and wanted to sleep while he could.

It took him a while to doze off, though. Questions still nagged at his brain. Who was Barker? Did the attempt on his life have anything to do with Dave Donaldson's disappearance? It seemed reasonable to Fargo to assume that if Barker was somehow involved with Dave's disappearance, he might not want anyone to go poking around in the matter . . . especially if Dave had been murdered and Barker wanted to cover up the crime.

But that theory didn't answer the question of how Barker had found out Fargo was on his way to Fort Smith. If Fargo believed Lydia's story, then Barker's involvement was still a mystery.

But if Lydia's story was a lie . . .

Well, then, in that case he might be riding right into a trap, Fargo thought. If so, it wouldn't be the first time. Sometimes the best way to turn the tables on a gang of plotters was to make them think they were about to win.

Fargo finally drifted into a deep, dreamless, refreshing sleep. He woke up before dawn the next morning, got up and pulled on his buckskins, and went out to the stable behind the hotel to check on the Ovaro. Not many people were moving around Fort Smith at this early hour.

44

The stallion was glad to see Fargo. A day's rest after the ride from St. Louis had restored the big horse's vigor and enthusiasm. Fargo could tell that the Ovaro was ready to hit the trail again.

When he stepped into the hotel dining room a short time later, he found Grady Donaldson waiting for him at one of the tables. A coffeepot already sat on the table, and steam rose from the black brew in the cup sitting in front of Grady. He grinned at Fargo and said, "I ordered a big breakfast for both of us. Figured you'd want to eat hearty before you start off."

Fargo pulled back a chair and returned the grin. "You're right about that," he told his old friend.

Grady became more serious. "Have you found out anything about Dave?"

Fargo hesitated, unsure whether to tell Grady about Devil's Den. Surely, if Grady had ever heard of the place in connection with Dave, he would have mentioned it. Yet Fargo wanted to be certain of that.

"Don't get your hopes up," he cautioned, "but I may have turned up something."

Grady leaned forward. "What is it? Tell me," he said eagerly.

"Have you ever heard of a place called Devil's Den?"

Grady's forehead creased in a frown. "Devil's Den?" he repeated, clearly thinking hard about it, trying to dredge up a memory of the name from his brain. But after a moment he shook his head and said, "No, I can't say as I have. What is it, Skye? Do you think Dave is there?"

"There's an indication that he might have been headed for there when he left Fort Smith."

"An indication? What the hell kind of talk is that? Give it to me straight, Skye. What's this all about?"

"I've told you all I know, Grady," Fargo said. "Somebody told me they'd overheard Dave mention the place. That's it."

Other than the details of Lydia's identity, Fargo had told Grady the truth. Grady chewed it over and finally

45

nodded. "Fair enough. And that's already more than I found out in weeks of asking around town about Dave." His enthusiasm returned. "I knew I did the right thing by sending for you. You're going to find him, I just know it!"

Fargo smiled and poured himself a cup of coffee. He was glad Grady was optimistic again. A little optimism couldn't hurt anyone.

The breakfast of flapjacks, bacon, eggs, and hash browns, all washed down with several cups of coffee, finished the job of restoring Fargo's strength. He felt as anxious to hit the trail as the Ovaro did.

Grady tagged along with him as he went across the street to a store and replenished his supplies. Grady insisted on paying for the provisions as well. "I know better than to offer you money for doing me a favor, Skye," he said, "but the least you can do is let me take care of your expenses."

Fargo didn't argue with that. He filled up his saddlebags, and Grady laid a double eagle on the store's counter.

The sun peeked over the hills to the east as Fargo led the saddled stallion from the stable and slung the saddlebags over the horse's back. He had plenty of ammunition for the Colt, and for the Henry rifle that rode in a fringed sheath attached to the saddle. He was ready to go, and he saw no point in delaying.

For a second, he thought about Lydia Mallory. It would have been nice to bid her a proper farewell, but she probably wasn't awake yet this morning. Fargo grinned to himself as he thought that such things would just have to wait until he got back to Fort Smith. Then Lydia could give him a proper hello, preferably between some nice clean sheets.

Fargo swung up into the saddle and then reached down to grasp Grady Donaldson's hand. "I'll do the best I can," he told his old friend as they shook hands.

"I know that," Grady said in a voice thick with

emotion. "Thanks, Skye. I know if anybody can find my son, you're the man for the job."

Fargo wheeled the Ovaro around, lifted a hand in a gesture of farewell, and rode out of Fort Smith.

He crossed the Arkansas River on a long, high bridge that slanted down from the bluff to the lowlands on the other side of the river. The main road followed the river, but a smaller trail slanted off to the northwest, toward Tahlequah. Fargo had visited that settlement before and knew it was several days' ride from Fort Smith.

Most folks had the wrong idea about the Indians who lived in the Nations, he mused, as he jogged along easily on the Ovaro. They were called the Five Civilized Tribes—the Cherokee, Chickasaw, Choctaw, Creek, and Seminole—and they lived in cabins and farmed pretty much like white settlers. Thirty years earlier, the government had pushed them out of their homelands in the southeastern United States and sent them to live on reservations in Indian Territory. That long pilgrimage was fittingly called the Trail of Tears.

Fargo didn't blame the Indians for shedding some tears along that trail. They had been uprooted from their homes and forced to travel hundreds of miles to a new, unknown place. Much of the land in Indian Territory really wasn't that bad, and once they got there, they were able to resume their lives. But to the ones who had grown up elsewhere, it wasn't home and never would be.

The army had small posts at Fort Gibson and Fort Towson, but they did little to enforce law and order in the Nations. Each of the tribes had its own police force, sometimes called Lighthorsemen, but their jurisdiction extended only to members of their own tribe. The Indian police couldn't do anything about the white outlaws who had fled into the territory from neighboring states. As Fargo had told Lydia, it was a raw, rugged, lawless land, but at the same time, it was a beautiful land, dotted with wooded hills and bluffs and watered by numerous creeks and rivers.

Fargo let the stallion set his own pace. The big black-and-white horse settled into his usual ground-eating lope. From time to time, Fargo stopped to rest his mount, though the Ovaro didn't need much rest. At midday, he paused longer and ate some jerky while the stallion grazed on the grass along a creek bank. Fargo propped his back against a tree trunk as he gnawed on the dried, jerked beef.

While he sat there, apparently at his ease, his eyes scanned the low, rolling hills around him and his ears listened for the sound of hoofbeats. He didn't hear anything, but his eyes caught a flicker of movement on a hilltop behind him, along the way from which he had come. He wasn't sure, but he thought it was a rider.

Fargo's eyes narrowed. He watched the area closely as he chewed the jerky, but he didn't see anything else.

He knew better than to think he had imagined the distant rider—he didn't make mistakes like that. But just because someone else was using this trail, it didn't mean that he was being followed. Whoever was back there might have a perfectly legitimate reason for riding toward Tahlequah.

Or it might be the mysterious Barker, looking for another chance to bushwhack him.

Fargo was already in the habit of being careful. Now that he knew someone was behind him, he would be more alert than ever.

He rode on through the afternoon and camped that night beside another stream. The Ovaro would wake him if anyone came nosing around the camp. Fargo rolled up in his blankets and went to sleep, with his head pillowed on his saddle.

In the morning he got another early start. By noon he hadn't seen any further signs of anyone following him. Either nobody was back there anymore, or the follower had gotten more careful.

That afternoon he spotted a wagon on the trail in

front of him, about half a mile ahead. The vehicle was headed in the same direction, but it moved much more slowly. Fargo knew he would catch up to the wagon in short order.

Before he got there, however, gunshots suddenly rang out. Fargo leaned forward in the saddle as he saw several riders sweep out of the trees alongside the road. They fell in behind the wagon, still shooting, as the driver whipped his team into a frantic run.

Fargo didn't like the looks of this. He didn't know anything about the driver of the wagon or the men who were chasing him, but he didn't like to see a man outnumbered and outgunned. He heeled the Ovaro into a gallop. The big stallion leaped forward eagerly.

Up ahead, the wagon careened around a bend in the trail. Fargo thought for a second that it was going to turn over. The bushwhackers continued to close the gap. On the wagon seat, the driver hunched as low as possible to make himself a smaller target.

Fargo slid the Henry from its sheath as he guided the stallion with his knees. He brought the repeating rifle to his shoulder, levered a cartridge into the chamber, and squeezed off a shot. He didn't figure to hit anything from the back of a running horse, but he thought he could come close enough to the bushwhackers to maybe spook them.

They must have heard the flat crack of the Henry and the whine of the bullet as it passed over their heads. A couple of the men pulled rein and turned around hurriedly to see where this new threat was coming from. Fargo saw powder smoke puff from the barrels of their pistols, but he didn't worry—the range was still too great for a handgun.

Not for a rifle, though. Now that he had their attention, he reined the stallion to a halt and drew a bead. His next shot kicked up dirt near the hooves of one of the horses. The animals danced around skittishly and caused their riders to stop shooting. The men had their hands full maintaining control of the horses.

Fargo levered the Henry and fired again. A hat leaped from the head of one of the men. He heard them curse as they pulled their horses around, yelled at their companions, and then fled into the trees. The other men broke off the pursuit and followed them, vanishing into the woods.

The wagon never slowed down. It went out of sight around another bend in the trail.

Fargo sent the stallion loping ahead again. He kept the Henry ready, just in case the bushwhackers doubled back and made another try for him or the wagon.

He wanted to catch up to the wagon, let the driver know he was safe, and maybe find out what it was all about. It was really none of his affair, of course, but he had made it his business when he took a hand in the fight.

He rode hard, reached the bend in the trail, rounded it and then another one a hundred yards farther on. He saw the wagon up ahead and was surprised to note that it had stopped. The driver was nowhere to be seen. Fargo wondered if perhaps the man had been wounded and had fallen off his seat. He kept an eye out along the edges of the trail but didn't see a body anywhere.

The thick growth came up close to the trail on both sides. Maybe the driver had decided to abandon his vehicle and hide out until he was sure it was safe. Fargo called, "Hello?" as he rode up to the wagon. The back was open, but it carried some sort of bulky cargo covered with a large sheet of canvas.

A gun made a cracking sound somewhere closeby. Fargo heard a slug sizzle past his head.

He left the saddle in a rolling dive that carried him behind the nearest wagon wheel. The vehicle provided some cover. The Henry was still in Fargo's hands. He held it tightly as he called out, "Hold your fire! I'm a friend!"

He heard a rustling in the woods and raised his head enough to peer over the back of the wagon.

What appeared to be a slender man in denim trousers, a gray woolen shirt, a brown vest, and a battered old black hat stepped from the trees and pointed a single-shot rifle at Fargo. Fargo had no doubt the rifle had been reloaded since that first shot.

He stepped out from behind the wagon and held the Henry well away from his body. His other hand was empty and in plain sight. "Take it easy," Fargo said. "I'm not looking for trouble. In fact, I'm the one who ran off those bushwhackers."

"Much obliged," the wagon driver said, "but you'll forgive me if I don't trust you right off."

Fargo's eyes widened a little with a look of surprise. The voice belonged to a woman.

Now that he looked closer, he could see the gentle swell of small breasts under the vest, and he noticed that the slender hips had a womanly curve to them that would have been more obvious if the trousers had been tighter. Thick, dark hair was tucked under the old black hat. The woman's face was slender, like the rest of her, and her bronzed skin, high cheekbones, and flashing dark eyes revealed her Indian heritage. Now that Fargo had gotten a better look at her, he realized she was quite attractive.

But still dangerous—the steady way she held the rifle was proof of that.

"My name is Skye Fargo," he said. He had found that sometimes people were less inclined to shoot if they knew the name of the person they were pointing a gun at.

Sure enough, the young woman lowered the rifle a little but still pointed it in Fargo's general direction. "Thank you for your help, Mr. Fargo."

"Who were those men? Why were they after you?"

A faint smile curved the woman's lips. "I believe that's my business, not yours."

She spoke well, which came as no surprise to Fargo. He pegged her as a Cherokee, and he knew how highly her people valued education. One of the old chiefs, a man named Sequoya, had even devised a Cherokee alphabet and system of writing. One of the first things the tribe had done, after being forced by the army to migrate westward, was to establish schools on the reservation.

Fargo shrugged and said, "All right. If you don't want to tell me, I reckon that's your right. Are you headed for Tahlequah?"

"Perhaps."

"So am I. I could ride along with you, in case those fellas come back and try to cause more trouble for you."

"That won't be necessary," she said crisply. "I appreciate your help, Mr. Fargo, but I can take care of myself from here on out."

"I'm not sure you could have if those men had caught up to you. A single-shot rifle against half a dozen six-shooters isn't very good odds."

"Thank you, again," she said. Clearly, she didn't want to discuss the matter, and she didn't want Fargo's company.

He wasn't going to force himself on her. He gave her a nod and caught up the Ovaro's reins. "I'll be riding on, then," he said.

She made no reply.

Fargo swung up into the saddle and loped off up the trail, still headed toward Tahlequah. He glanced back over his shoulder once and saw that the woman had climbed onto the seat and gotten the wagon rolling again. Maybe she didn't want to travel with him, he thought, but she couldn't stop him from staying fairly closeby. If he heard more gunfire, he could turn around and get back to her in a hurry.

But there wasn't any more shooting. That night, as he sat in his camp and sipped coffee, he saw the tiny glow of her campfire a half mile or so behind him. She could have caught up easily and shared his fire, but it was her choice not to do so.

The night passed quietly. As Fargo arose the next

morning, he knew that, with luck, he would reach Tahlequah on this day. He wished he had asked the young woman about Devil's Den when he talked to her the day before, but he hadn't thought of it.

Given her attitude, she probably wouldn't have told him anything anyway, he thought.

Since there had been trouble, he was doubly alert as he rode on toward the Cherokee settlement. The young woman was still behind him with her wagon, and he tried to keep an eye on her as well.

Not even the Trailsman could see everything, but his keen ears did pick up a crackle in the brush just before several men burst out of the trees at around midmorning and trained rifles on him. Fargo reined in sharply. His hand hovered close to the butt of the Colt. If the men started shooting, he planned to draw the revolver and take as many of them with him as he could before they cut him down.

The men held their fire, though, and one of them called out to him, "Don't move, mister!"

Since it didn't seem that they intended to murder him out of hand, Fargo was willing to talk to them. "What's this all about?" he asked in a flinty tone of voice that showed he wasn't happy to have guns pointed at him.

"We're Cherokee Lighthorsemen, the law in these parts," the spokesman for the group said. "So we'll ask the questions."

Fargo frowned. "I haven't broken any laws that I know of."

"You're white," said one of the other men. "That means you're probably an outlaw."

With an effort, Fargo controlled his temper. He didn't like for anyone to jump to conclusions about him. He said, "You've got me wrong, mister. I'm the law-abiding sort."

"Yeah? What's your name?"

"Fargo. Skye Fargo."

He saw that the spokesman for the Cherokee lawmen recognized his name, or at least found it familiar. Before they could discuss the matter any further, the wagon came along the trail with a rattle of wheels.

The woman drew her team of draft horses to a stop and surveyed the scene on the trail ahead of her. With a smile, she said, "What's this, George? Have you caught yourself a desperado?"

The spokesman lowered his rifle and smiled, and Fargo saw right away that he was fond of the woman. "I don't know what he is, Alma, other than white. Says his name is Fargo. You know him?" .

"We met yesterday," the young woman called Alma replied. "He gave me a hand when some of Abel Gannon's men tried to steal my grandfather's wagon."

George lowered his rifle even more and looked at Fargo with new respect. "Is that right?" He motioned to the other men. "Take it easy, boys. It looks like we were wrong about Mr. Fargo here." He looked at Fargo and went on, "I thought you were one of those gunmen Gannon keeps bringing in."

Fargo thought he understood now. Evidently, a gang of white outlaws had moved into the area and caused trouble for the Cherokee who lived here. He supposed he didn't blame the Lighthorsemen for thinking he could be one of them.

He wasn't clear on one thing, however, so he said, "I thought the tribal police only had jurisdiction over members of the Cherokee Nation."

George had started to smile, but that expression vanished and was replaced by a scowl. "Some of us don't like to stand by and do nothing while our people are robbed and killed."

"Maybe you should send word to the army over at Fort Gibson." To a certain extent, Fargo was playing devil's advocate, and he knew it. He didn't blame these people for wanting to take care of themselves, and he had little patience for the folderol that was involved in dealing with the army and the Bureau of Indian Affairs.

"The army's not interested in protecting us from the white men," one of the other men snapped, "only in protecting the white men from us."

"Well, I can't say as I blame you for being upset," Fargo told them. "Reckon I would be, too. But I'm not here to cause any trouble for you, and I'd appreciate being allowed to go on my way."

George nodded. He said, "Sure, since Alma vouches for you." He turned to the others. "Ben, go get our horses." He tucked his rifle under his arm and came over to Fargo. As he extended his hand, he said, "I'm George Dayton."

Fargo shook his hand. George was a dark, stockily built man. Like the other Lighthorsemen, he dressed in what could almost be considered a white man's clothes. The red sashes the men wore around their waists, in place of belts, were the only difference.

George nodded toward the wagon. "You already know Alma Cloudwalker."

Fargo smiled at the woman. "We haven't been introduced, but yep, we've met." He didn't mention that she had held a gun on him during most of their previous conversation.

She didn't bring that up, either. "Mr. Fargo," she said politely, and he reached up to touch a finger to the brim of his hat.

The other Lighthorsemen came out of the woods, leading their horses. As they mounted up, George said to Alma, "If you're headed for Tahlequah, maybe we ought to ride with you. Especially since Gannon has already tried to grab your wagon."

"I can take care of myself, George," she said, and Fargo had the feeling that the two of them had had this discussion before.

"No, we can get back to our patrol later," George said stubbornly. "You never know what that bunch from Devil's Den will do."

5

Fargo tried not to show the sudden interest he felt at George Dayton's statement. Keeping his voice casual, he asked, "Devil's Den? What's that?"

George glanced at him. "A place north of here, in some hills where those white outlaws I mentioned hide out. It's not worth your life to go there, Mr. Fargo, so I wouldn't advise it."

A bad feeling suddenly came over Fargo. "This Abel Gannon—he's got a good-sized gang, does he?"

"They come and go, but there's always a dozen or more of them up there. Killers and cutthroats, every one."

And Dave Donaldson had been headed for Devil's Den, Fargo thought, at least according to Lydia Mallory. That meant he had either ridden in there unaware of what the place was and probably gotten himself killed . . .

Or else he was a member of Abel Gannon's gang of murderous desperadoes.

Fargo's heart sank at that thought. He didn't want to have to tell Grady Donaldson either of those things. Of the two, though, it might be better if the gang had murdered Dave. It would devastate Grady to learn that his son was an outlaw, Fargo thought. Such a thing just couldn't be.

And yet, how well did Grady really know his son? Not that well, Fargo thought. The two of them had been separated for quite a few years. Dave might have grown up not recognizing the difference between right and wrong. A lot of men turned bad, and there was often no way to know what had caused it.

"What's your interest in Devil's Den?" George asked.

Fargo shrugged. "Just curious. Sounds like a bad place, and from what you said, the name fits. I'll steer clear of it."

"That'd be wise." George turned his horse. "Come on, boys." He looked over his shoulder. "Mr. Fargo, are you riding with us?"

"Thanks," Fargo said. "I reckon I might as well."

The party set off, following the trail northwest toward Tahlequah. If Devil's Den were north of here, Fargo thought, that would put it between the settlement and the Arkansas line, in an especially rugged line of foothills that turned, farther east, into the Ozark Mountains.

George Dayton rode next to the wagon and tried to engage Alma Cloudwalker in conversation. Fargo noticed that Alma gave him mostly short answers. It looked like George was smitten with her, but she didn't return the feeling, though she was polite enough to the Lighthorseman. Once or twice, Fargo caught her glancing around to look at him. He wasn't vain enough to think that she was anything more than curious about him.

But he noticed that she looked away quickly whenever their eyes met, and that made him smile faintly to himself. If she was interested, then he was, too. She was certainly lovely.

He looked at the canvas-covered cargo in the back of the wagon and wondered what it was. The Cherokee were farmers, but it was too early in the season for a crop to be in already. Of course, what Alma hauled to Tahlequah was none of his business.

The other members of the Lighthorse patrol didn't seem too talkative. Fargo tried to drum up a conversation with the man who rode beside him. George had called him Ben, Fargo recalled.

Sensing that he wasn't going to get anywhere with subtlety, Fargo instead asked Ben a blunt question. "Do you know a fella named Dave Donaldson?"

Ben grunted. "A white man?"

"That's right."

"I don't pay much attention to white men. But I don't recall knowin' anybody by that name. He a friend of yours?"

"We have a mutual friend," Fargo replied. "He's supposed to be somewhere here in the Nations. Thought I'd look him up and say howdy."

"Indian Territory's a big place, mister. You'd have to narrow it down more than that."

"I heard he was headed for Tahlequah."

Again, Ben grunted disdainfully. "There's a few whites in the capital. You can ask around."

"Thanks," Fargo said. He rode along in silence for a moment, and then continued, "I was wondering, too, if there's a freight line that runs between there and Fort Smith."

"From Fort Smith to Tahlequah and back, you mean?" Ben looked over at him suspiciously. "If there is, I haven't heard of it. And I reckon I'd know, since we patrol this part of the territory pretty regularlike."

"I guess I was misinformed," Fargo said. Inside, he felt a mixture of anger and disappointment. Clearly, Dave's story about starting up a freight line had been a pack of lies. It was beginning to look more and more like he was mixed up in something shady. More than likely, he had joined up with Abel Gannon and the other outlaws who were plaguing the Cherokee Nation.

Fargo rode on in silence as he turned over grim thoughts in his mind. Speculation wasn't enough. He had to find Dave Donaldson and see for certain if Dave was riding with Gannon.

Then, if it was true, Fargo could think about how

he would tell Grady that his son had turned outlaw. The one thing he was almost completely certain of was that he wouldn't be sending good news to his old friend.

The sudden crack of a gunshot snapped Fargo out of his reverie. Close beside him, a man grunted in pain. Fargo looked around and saw Ben topple from the saddle. The Cherokee Lighthorseman clutched at his chest as he fell. Blood spurted between his fingers.

The shot had come from the woods beside the road, and hard on its heels came more blasts from the trees on both sides of the trail. Fargo and his companions had ridden into an ambush, and now they were trapped in a deadly crossfire.

The tribal policemen tried to return the fire. Another man was already dead. The left sleeve of George Dayton's coat was bloody where a bullet had grazed him. He shouted, "Alma, get down!" and reached over with his good hand to grab Alma's shoulder and shove her over the seat and into the back of the wagon.

Unfortunately, the shooting had frightened the team of horses, and without Alma's sure hands on the reins, the animals bolted, drawing the wagon after them.

George cried out, "Alma!" The Lighthorseman started after the wagon at a gallop. But after only a few steps, George's horse broke stride. The animal's front legs folded up underneath it as blood gushed from a wound in its throat. The horse tumbled forward on the trail, sending George sailing over its head.

Right then, Fargo would have gone after the wagon and tried to stop the team, but too many bullets buzzed around him like angry hornets. He palmed out his Colt and triggered three shots toward the woods as he swept the revolver in a short arc. He knew he might not hit anything, but he would give the ambushers something to think about.

He leaned forward over the stallion's neck to make himself a smaller target and sent the big horse leaping ahead. Fargo twisted in the saddle and let loose two more shots at the trees on the other side of the trail. That emptied the Colt, so he jammed it back into its holster. The Lighthorsemen had now started to put up a better fight, and the firing from the woods slacked off a little. Fargo rode through the hail of bullets and thundered after the runaway wagon.

He hated to see George and the other Lighthorsemen left behind to face the ambush, but he knew he was the only one who could catch up to the wagon before it crashed and put Alma's life in mortal danger. Already, the wagon was more than a hundred yards ahead of him. He saw Alma bouncing around the back of the out-of-control vehicle. He couldn't tell if she was conscious or had been knocked out by the jostling.

Fargo urged the Ovaro on to greater speed. The stallion responded gallantly. Fargo knew he could catch the wagon sooner or later. There was no way those draft horses could outrun the Ovaro. It was just a matter of time.

But that was time he might not have. An open field loomed to the left of the trail. For no good reason except that they were maddened with fright, the horses veered off the road and took off across the field. Fargo swung the stallion after them. His jaw tightened suddenly as he saw what was on the other side of the open ground.

One of the many creeks in the area had apparently cut a deep gully across the landscape. Trees grew on the far side of the gully, but the near side dropped off sheerly, with no warning and nothing to slow down the stampeding team. From where he was, Fargo couldn't tell how deep the gully was, but if the horses were unable to stop and the wagon and team plunged into the gully, it would be a terrible crash. The odds of Alma surviving it were small.

Fargo prodded the Ovaro, calling for every ounce of speed and stamina that the magnificent stallion possessed. The wind from their passage slapped at Fargo's face, even though he crouched low in the saddle. With every great bound, the stallion cut down the gap between him and the wagon.

Already, the team was too close to the gully for Fargo to try to stop it. He had planned to leap from the Ovaro's back into the wagon and retrieve the reins. He had accomplished such tricky, death-defying feats in the past. But there was no time now. The best he could hope to do was snatch Alma from the jaws of death.

"Alma!" he shouted as he closed in on the runaway vehicle, hoping that she was conscious and could hear him over the pounding hoofbeats of the team and the rattling of the wagon. "Alma!"

He saw her reach up, grasp the sideboard, and pull herself up from the wagon bed. Her hat had fallen off, and her long hair, as black as a raven's wing, flew around her head as the wind blew it. "Fargo!" she screamed, and then turned to cast a frantic glance at the gully toward which the wagon was rushing.

Fargo was now only a few yards away. He trusted the Ovaro to keep track of how close they were to the edge of the gully, and he watched Alma instead. She gripped the sideboard with one hand and extended the other arm toward him. He leaned to the side and reached for her as the stallion drew even with the wagon.

Close . . . just a little closer . . . *now!* he told himself as, with a lunge, he grasped Alma's wrist. He pulled hard, and she helped by leaping toward him. They came together in a bone-jarring collision. Fargo threw his other arm around her, and clamped his knees tightly against the stallion's heaving flanks to keep from falling out of the saddle.

At the same time, he felt the Ovaro twist and turn beneath him, and from the corner of his eye he saw the gully looming right beside them. Another few inches and they would have fallen in.

With screams of terror, the runaway horses plunged

over the brink and plummeted toward the stream, some twenty feet below. The wagon went after them. Its momentum caused it to seemingly float in midair for a second before it crashed down. The vehicle splintered and broke apart, and the cargo flew from the back and scattered everywhere.

Fargo now had Alma perched in front of him on the Ovaro. She clutched at him and trembled, still frightened out of her wits by the close call. The stallion slowed to a trot and then came to a stop on his own, a few feet from the edge of the gully. Fargo turned his head and looked down at the devastation.

The wagon was a total wreck. Four of the six horses in the team appeared to be dead. The other two writhed in pain and uttered shrill whinnies. Someone needed to climb down there and put them out of their misery, but right now he had his hands full.

"Oh, my God . . . oh, my God. . . ." Alma repeated. "I thought . . . oh, my God!"

"Take it easy," Fargo said to her soothingly. "It's all over now."

But as a matter of fact, he didn't know if it really was over. The battle might still be going on between the Cherokee Lighthorsemen and the killers who had bushwhacked them.

Cradling Alma in front of him, Fargo trotted back toward the site of the ambush. He listened for the sound of shots but didn't hear any. As they came closer, he shifted Alma and freed his right arm so that he could draw the Henry from its sheath. He hadn't had a chance to reload the Colt.

Before they reached the scene of the ambush, several riders hurried around a bend in the trail. Fargo was ready to open fire, but he lowered the Henry as he recognized George Dayton and the other tribal policemen. George cried out, "Alma!" and galloped forward. As he came up to Fargo, he asked anxiously, "Is she all right?"

Fargo nodded. "Just shaken up, I think. I haven't had a chance to check for injuries."

Alma wiped tears away from her bronzed cheeks. "I . . . I'm fine," she said. "But my grandfather's wagon . . . his horses . . ."

"They crashed in a gully back there a ways," Fargo explained as he saw the puzzled look on George's face. "I got Alma out of the wagon before it went over the edge."

"Thank God for that," George said fervently.

"How about you?" Fargo asked. He nodded toward George's bloody sleeve. "How bad are you hit?"

George looked down at the wound and then shrugged. The gesture made him wince in pain. "It hurts like blazes," he admitted, "but the slug just knocked a chunk of meat off my arm. I'll be all right." His face tightened in a look of rage. "But Ben and Asa—they're both dead. I got a couple more men wounded, too. Damn that Gannon!"

"You're sure it was him?"

"Who else could it be?"

"You tell me," Fargo said. "I'm new in these parts, remember?"

"It was Gannon," George declared. "He's the only one who's been raising hell around here. He and his men made their try for Alma's wagon yesterday, and you stopped them. Today they set a trap instead, and we rode right into it." His voice was filled with bitter self-recrimination. "Some lawmen we are."

Fargo wasn't very happy with himself, either. He should have noticed some warning sign of the ambush before the shooting started. But he wasn't going to waste time or energy brooding about it.

"The time will come to settle the score with Gannon," he said. "Right now, I think we'd better take Miss Cloudwalker and your wounded men on to Tahlequah, so they can get some medical attention."

George nodded that he agreed. "As soon as we load

the bodies on their horses. I'm not leaving my men out here for the buzzards and the wolves, and there's not time to bury them and still reach the settlement by dark."

They rode back up the trail and recovered the bodies of the men who had died in the gun battle. George explained to Fargo that the bushwhackers had fled after several minutes of furious firing.

"I guess we put up more of a fight than they expected," George said as the party once again started toward Tahlequah. "I don't reckon they counted on you being with us, either. From what little I saw before I was hit, it looked like you were doing some pretty good shooting." He hesitated for a second and then went on, "You're the one they call the Trailsman, aren't you?"

"Some folks do," Fargo admitted.

"I thought I recognized the name. You've been a friend to folks here in the Nations before, helped out the tribes when you could."

"I lend a hand wherever I can," Fargo said. "It's been a while since I've ridden down this way, though."

Alma rode behind him now, her arms around his waist. She had settled down quite a bit after her brush with death. She said, "I think I've heard my grandfather speak of you. His name is Jefferson Cloudwalker."

Fargo thought about it for a moment and then shook his head. "I don't recall the name."

"I don't think he ever knew you personally. I believe he said he had seen you at Fort Gibson a few times. He scouted for the army when he was younger."

Fargo nodded. "There's a good chance we were around there at the same time, then."

The riders reached the field where the wagon had left the trail. George sent a couple of men over to the gully to check on the horses and finish off the injured ones if necessary. However, the Lighthorsemen rode back a few minutes later and reported that all of the horses had succumbed to their injuries.

Fargo felt a shudder go through Alma when she heard this news. "Grandfather loved those horses," she murmured.

"One more score to settle with Gannon," George said in a hard, angry voice.

Several times during the day, Fargo saw George glance over at him and Alma. He figured the Lighthorseman wished Alma was riding with him rather than with Fargo. George didn't say anything about it, though. And he had other things to worry about besides romance, including the fact that his patrol had been ambushed and two of his men killed, not to mention the wound in his arm, which had a bloodstained, makeshift bandage tied around it.

Late that afternoon, they rode past the small village of Park Hill, where the home of John Ross, the chief of the Cherokee Nation, was located. Ross had been one of the leaders of the Cherokee for many years and was a rather controversial political figure, but Fargo knew him to be a good man who cared more about his people than anything else.

Tahlequah lay just a few miles beyond Park Hill, where the Illinois and the Barren Fork rivers came together. It was by far the largest settlement in Indian Territory, and boasted close to two thousand citizens. As Fargo and his companions rode along the main street, he was again struck by how much Tahlequah resembled any other good-sized frontier settlement, with numerous stores, hotels, and shops, along with the buildings that housed the government of the Cherokee Nation. Anyone who rode in here expecting to see lodges or wickiups, just because it was an Indian town, would be disappointed.

One major difference between Tahlequah and a white settlement was obvious right away: there were no saloons in Tahlequah. Whiskey was not allowed in the Nations.

George pointed out one of the hotels to Fargo and said, "That's the best place to stay. You'll be around town for a few days, in case my captain wants to ask you any questions about what happened today, won't you?"

Fargo nodded. "I'm in no hurry. I'll be around."

"You know, you never did tell me what you're doing in these parts," George said.

Fargo recalled that he had been talking about that with Ben just before the unfortunate Lighthorseman was killed in the ambush. George wouldn't have heard any of that conversation, however, because he had been too busy talking to Alma.

"I'm looking for a white man named Dave Donaldson," Fargo said. "He was interested in starting a business here in Tahlequah."

"I don't know him," George replied with a frown. "But there are a lot of mixed-bloods and whites who have married into the tribe around here."

Dave wasn't a mixed-blood, nor had he married a Cherokee woman, at least as far as Fargo knew. He had to admit, though, that he didn't know what Dave might have done in the months since Grady had seen him last.

"We need to take these bodies to the undertaker and then report to the captain," George went on. He lifted a hand in a farewell to Fargo and then said to Alma, "Are you sure you're all right? There's nothing I can do for you?"

"I'm fine now, George," she told him. "Just upset about what happened to my grandfather's wagon and goods. I'll tell Mr. Dupree about it and then get a room for the night at the hotel. Maybe I can rent a horse tomorrow and start back home."

Fargo looked across the street and saw the name "Dupree" on one of the stores, a general mercantile that took up nearly an entire block. Whatever Alma's cargo had been, he supposed that she had intended to sell it to the store's proprietor.

George and the other tribal policemen rode on.

Fargo dismounted and helped Alma down, and then tied the Ovaro at the hitch rail in front of the hotel. Alma turned to him and said, "Thank you for everything, Mr. Fargo. I see now that I should have trusted you right from the start."

"Nothing wrong with being careful," Fargo told her. "Caution is one thing that keeps a person alive out here on the frontier." He grinned and nodded toward the general store. "Since you've decided I'm trustworthy, I thought I'd walk across the street with you and keep you company."

She smiled back at him. "That would be fine."

She had warmed up considerably since he'd met her, probably due to a combination of things. He had saved her life, and then they had spent hours riding in close proximity on the back of the Ovaro. It was hard to be standoffish with a person after something like that.

Fargo's grin broadened as he remembered how her small but firm breasts had felt as they rubbed against his back through their clothing. The Ovaro had a mighty smooth gait, but there was still a certain amount of swaying involved.

The street was broad, dusty, and dotted with piles of dung left behind by the numerous horses and mules that moved along it. Fargo cupped a hand under Alma's elbow to help her navigate a path to the store. Dusk had begun to settle over the town, but Dupree's Emporium was brightly lit. Fargo and Alma climbed a short flight of stairs to the combination porch and loading dock in front of the store.

They went inside and walked between shelves stacked with all sorts of goods, toward a long counter that ran across the rear of the big, high-ceilinged room. Several clerks in aprons stood behind the counter and waited on customers. A man in an expensive black suit was behind the counter as well, and when he saw Alma he smiled at first. Then a look of suspicion and concern appeared on his face as he noticed Fargo beside her.

"Alma, my dear, it's good to see you, as always," the man said as Fargo and Alma reached the counter. "Who's your friend?"

"This is Mr. Fargo," Alma said. "There was some trouble on the way into town, Mr. Dupree, and he helped me."

"Trouble? Trouble, you say?" Dupree was perhaps thirty-five years old, a handsome man with curly brown hair that had a light touch of gray, and a short beard that was the same shade.

"Abel Gannon's men tried to steal my grandfather's wagon yesterday."

"My God!" Dupree exclaimed. "Are you all right, Alma?"

"Yes, of course. Mr. Fargo came along and stopped them, but today they ambushed us again, when we were riding with George Dayton and his Lighthorse patrol. Two men were killed, and the wagon was wrecked in a gully when the team ran away. I would have died if not for Mr. Fargo."

"Then we all owe the gentleman a great debt." Dupree thrust his hand across the counter. "I'm Simon Dupree, Mr. Fargo. It's an honor to meet you."

Fargo shook hands with him. He didn't like Simon Dupree. The man struck him as pompous and self-confident to the point of arrogance. But Fargo was polite anyway and nodded to Dupree as they shook.

"You say it was Abel Gannon and his men who waylaid you?" Dupree asked as he turned his attention back to Alma.

"That's right."

"The man's perfidy knows no bounds! Is there no limit to his lawlessness?"

"Somebody will stop him sooner or later," Fargo said quietly. "Justice always catches up to those who live outside the law."

"A noble sentiment," Dupree said, "and one which I wish I could agree with. But I'm not convinced that the law will ever catch up to Abel Gannon. Not as long as George Dayton is in charge of things."

"George is a good man," Alma said quickly. "He does the best he can."

"Hmmph. I'm not sure it's good enough." Dupree shook his head. "I'm sorry to hear about Jefferson's wagon. Were all the goods lost as well?"

"Everything," Alma said. "The kegs were all busted to pieces."

"That's a damned shame, if you'll pardon my language. Jefferson Cloudwalker's hives produce the best honey in the territory. The best in this whole part of the country, I daresay."

So that was it, Fargo thought. The back of the wagon had been filled with kegs of honey. That creek water must have been mighty sweet for a while as all the honey from the busted kegs flowed into it.

A door behind the counter then opened, and a woman stepped out of the store's back room. Fargo glanced at her and then looked again, impressed by her beauty.

While Alma Cloudwalker was a lovely young woman, this newcomer, a few years older than Alma, was breathtaking. Waves of midnight-black hair were parted in the center of her head, and framed a heart-shaped face with exotically dark eyes. She wore a dark blue dress that hugged the proud thrust of her breasts and the graceful curves of her hips and legs. Her lips were full and naturally red, and she smiled as she came over to Simon Dupree and placed a hand on his arm in a possessive gesture.

"Alma, dear," she murmured. "So good to see you again."

Fargo noted the wedding ring on this woman's finger. He had already decided that Dupree was white, not of mixed blood. Therefore, it was likely that he was married to a woman with Cherokee blood. Clearly this newcomer was his wife.

"Hello, Mrs. Dupree," Alma said, confirming Fargo's guess. "I was just telling your husband that Abel Gannon wrecked my grandfather's wagon on the way into town. All the honey was lost."

The woman's eyes, so large and dark that it appeared that a man could topple into them and get lost forever, widened in a look of surprise. "What? All gone? All of it?"

Dupree patted her hand. "There, there, my dear. Don't worry. That's one good thing about honey—as long as Jefferson has his hives, his bees can make more."

"Yes, I suppose so. Still, this is a terrible thing. Were you hurt, Alma?"

"No, ma'am."

Fargo thought he saw a flash of irritation in the other woman's eyes. She probably didn't like being called "ma'am." It made her seem older than she was.

"Thank goodness for that," Mrs. Dupree went on. "Someone should do something about Abel Gannon. A bullet or a hang rope would be just fine."

Dupree laughed. "My, aren't you the bloodthirsty one, Eva?"

"It's no more than Abel Gannon deserves," Eva Dupree said. She looked at Fargo, as she was clearly curious about his identity, but she didn't ask who he was and her husband didn't volunteer to make any introductions.

"Well, I just wanted to let you know what happened," Alma said. "I'm going to go over to the hotel and get a room for the night."

"That's not necessary. I'm sure we could find room for you," Dupree offered.

If he saw the slitted look his wife gave him, he made no sign of it. Fargo noticed, though.

Alma seemed a little uncomfortable as she said hurriedly, "No, that's all right. Thank you, though."

"You're sure—?" Dupree began.

"She said so, darling," Eva chimed in, her hand tightening on her husband's arm.

"Of course. But if you need anything, Alma . . ."

"I'll let you know, Mr. Dupree," she promised.

"Good evening, Mr. Fargo," Dupree added, nodding to the Trailsman.

Fargo returned the nod and touched the brim of his hat as he looked at Mrs. Dupree. She favored him with a cool smile.

"Well, *that* was interesting," Alma said under her breath as she and Fargo left the emporium.

"Are those two always like that?"

"Most of the time." She looked up at him as they started across the street toward the hotel. "I was thinking . . . since we're both going to be staying here . . . perhaps we should have dinner together."

Fargo glanced over at her. It was difficult to tell, with her copper-colored skin, but he thought she was blushing—and prettily, at that.

"That sounds like a good idea," he said, and meant it. He could certainly think of worse ways to spend an evening.

And there was no way to predict how it would turn out, which made it all the more intriguing . . .

6

Over dinner, after they had both registered at the hotel, Alma Cloudwalker told Fargo about her family and how they had come to live in Indian Territory.

"My grandfather was on the Trail of Tears with Chief John Ross," she said. "They had been friends as boys and young men, but they split over the federal government's relocation policy. Chief Ross opposed the efforts to move the Five Civilized Tribes from our homeland in the southeast. My grandfather didn't like what was happening, either, but he thought the only alternative to cooperation was to fight a war with the United States that would destroy our people in the end. Of course, later on, the army *did* force the tribes to move, but there was no war. Chief Ross changed his stance and went along with those who advised cooperation, like my grandfather. They saved the Cherokee people."

"At the cost of your homes," Fargo pointed out.

"I was born here in the Nations. I've never known any other home."

He nodded and said, "I reckon that would make a difference, all right." Still, he could understand how some of the Cherokee might always harbor some resentment against the government that had uprooted them.

"It hasn't been a bad life. The worst part was that

my parents both died of a fever when I was young. My grandfather raised me after that. I didn't have any brothers or sisters, so it was just the two of us."

"Must have been lonely," Fargo said as he looked across the table at her.

"Sometimes it was," she admitted with a wistful sound in her voice. "But we stayed busy most of the time with the crops and Grandfather's hives. We've always made several trips into town each year. I came alone this time, though, because Grandfather's rheumatism has gotten worse. He didn't think he could stand the long ride."

Fargo nodded. "And you ran into trouble not once, but twice."

Alma laughed, but the sound didn't hold much humor. "That's right. Grandfather will probably never let me go anywhere alone again." She smiled at Fargo. "So I have to make the most of my opportunities."

Now, what did she mean by *that*? Fargo asked himself. He was pretty sure he knew the answer, but he planned to wait and see how things worked out. He didn't want to rush things.

They continued to chat as they ate. The food was good, and after being on the trail for several days, Fargo enjoyed having a hot meal. When they were finished, Alma said, "I suppose we'd better turn in now." She caught her breath and went on hurriedly, "I mean, go up to our . . . our rooms. Or at least, I should. You can do whatever you want, Mr. Fargo."

"What I want is for you to call me Skye."

"Oh. All right." She smiled again. "Skye. The name suits you."

"Thanks. I reckon I'll turn in, too."

"Then we can walk up together."

They left the hotel's dining room and went through the lobby and up the stairs to the second floor. Fargo's room was in the front, with Alma's across the hall. They had gone up earlier, briefly, before eating. Fargo had left his rifle and saddlebags in the room. The rest of his gear was down in the livery barn, where he had stabled the Ovaro for the night.

Alma hesitated at her door. "I guess this is good night," she said tentatively.

Fargo nodded, willing to let her play it any way she wanted. "I guess."

"I just wish . . ." She stopped short.

After a moment, Fargo said quietly, "You wish what, Alma?"

She moved closer to him, slender, coltish, a trifle awkward but undeniably lovely. "I wish you'd kiss me, Skye," she said in a rush, clearly wanting to get the words out before she lost her nerve.

Fargo smiled and said gently, "I think that would be mighty nice."

She came naturally into his arms and reached up to wrap her arms around his neck. Her eyes closed as she tipped her head back. Fargo's lips brushed hers, softly at first and then pressing down with more heat and urgency. She returned the kiss with equal ardor.

Fargo liked the feel of her body, strong like a willow wand, as she pressed against him. He couldn't help contrasting her slender figure with the more lush charms of Lydia Mallory that he had enjoyed back in Fort Smith a few days earlier. That is one of the wonderful things about women, he reflected, as her lips parted under his and he stroked her tongue—they come in all shapes and sizes and personalities, and Skye Fargo enjoyed just about all of them.

Alma thrust her pelvis against the hardness at his groin. After a second she pulled back and broke the kiss. He saw a mixed look of uncertainty and passion on her face. "You must think I . . . I'm awful," she gasped.

Fargo put a finger under her chin. "Nope. That thought never entered my mind."

"But only a brazen woman would do such a thing."

"There's nothing wrong with being brazen at the

right time and place," Fargo told her. "I reckon the world would be a lot better off if more people understood that."

"Then . . . then you think we should . . ."

"I think we should do whatever you want," Fargo said.

That simple statement caused a new boldness to show in her eyes. "Then I think you should make love to me," she declared.

"That sounds like the best idea I've heard in a long time," Fargo said.

They went into his room. Fargo drew the curtains across the single window and then lit the lamp on the table beside the bed. He turned the wick low so that it cast a warm yellow glow. When he turned toward Alma, he found that she had already taken off her vest and started to unbutton her shirt.

When she was finished with the buttons, she opened the shirt to reveal her smooth torso. Her breasts swelled modestly and were crowned with small, dark brown nipples. She dropped the shirt on the floor and murmured, "Your turn, Skye."

Fargo had already tossed his hat aside. Now he unbuckled his gunbelt and coiled it on the chair. He peeled the buckskin shirt over his head. Alma came closer to him and reached out to touch his muscular chest.

"So strong," she said, "but so many scars. Many people must have hurt you."

"Never so bad that I didn't recover from it," Fargo said. It was true that there had been much pain in his past, but he had never been the sort of man to look back. He always looked to the future instead, and right now, the immediate future looked mighty nice indeed. He put his arms around Alma's waist and pulled her to him. Her erect nipples prodded his chest as he kissed her again.

This time her tongue boldly invaded his mouth. He returned the heated caress. His hands slipped under the waistband of her trousers and explored the gentle swell of her hips. He cupped the cheeks of her rump, and that caused her to grind against him again.

Fargo slid her trousers down over her thighs while she worked at the buttons of his trousers. His erection throbbed impatiently, and when she finally freed it and wrapped her fingers around the long, thick shaft, Fargo's jaw tightened in pleasure. She stroked his manhood as she broke the kiss and leaned her head against his shoulder.

"You are so large, Skye. I . . . I don't know if it will fit." She gave a mischievous laugh. "But we will find out."

Damned right they would, he thought. And he hoped it would be soon.

Not too soon, though. First, there were a few other things he wanted to do. He slipped a hand between her thighs and found the wet heat of the crevice where her legs came together. He stroked the folds of flesh, and his touch brought a gasp of joy from her. After a few moments, Fargo embraced her and kissed her again, steering her toward the bed as he did so. She lay back and invitingly spread her legs wide.

Fargo accepted, but perhaps not in the way she expected, at least not right away. He knelt between her thighs and lowered his head to her sex. His tongue speared into her and made her hips buck upward as she gave a low, ecstatic cry. His tongue delved as deep as it could, and then he moved up to a little bud of flesh and sucked it between his lips. She gasped, closed her thighs around his head, and pumped her femininity against his face. A shudder ran through her as a swift, unexpected climax gripped her.

Fargo didn't put off his own pleasure any longer. As her spasms subsided and she sank back on the bed, he moved over her, poised between her thighs. He put the head of his shaft against her opening. A surge of his hips drove the length of him into her. She grabbed him around the neck and hung on for dear life as he penetrated her to the hilt.

With the need for release spurring him on, Fargo pumped hard, in and out of her. He sensed that her arousal was building again and knew that if he were able to hold off for a few minutes, he could bring her to another peak. He concentrated on that. His iron will allowed him to keep going until Alma jerked and trembled and cried out beneath him. The grip of her arms and legs around him tightened even more with the strength of her culmination.

Fargo then allowed his own climax to sweep over him. He poured himself into her, and each throbbing explosion shook him to his core. After what seemed almost like an eternity, it came to an end. Now breathless, with his heart thundering in his chest, he braced himself on his elbows so that his weight wouldn't crush her slender form. His lake-blue eyes looked down into her dark brown ones, and he saw that they were brimming with tears. She wasn't upset, though—he could tell that by the way she smiled and began to give him quick, sweet kisses.

"Skye," she said between those kisses, "I . . . I never knew . . . never knew it could be like that." She ducked her head shyly. "Was I all right?"

He laughed, the sound coming from deep within him. "You were more than all right," he told her. He kissed her forehead, her nose. "You were wonderful."

"Thank you. I . . . I don't have much experience . . ."

"It's not the experience you have," Fargo said. "It's what's in your heart."

"Oh, Skye," she whispered. She held him tightly again.

Fargo rolled onto his back. Alma snuggled against his side, and he put both arms around her and held her. They dozed off like that, and later in the night, when they woke up, they made love again—it was long and slow and sweet—and then once again they drifted off to sleep in each other's arms.

He had to go to Devil's Den. No matter how much Fargo thought about it, he didn't see any other answer to his problem. However, that wasn't the only problem he had at the moment.

He also had a stubborn young woman on his hands.

That morning, Alma looked at Fargo across the table in the hotel dining room where they were having breakfast. "You don't understand, Skye," she said. "I have to get back home. Grandfather's there by himself, and he doesn't get around as well as he used to."

"Those outlaws have come after you twice," Fargo pointed out. "If you're by yourself and you cross paths with them again, it's liable to be bad."

Her chin came up defiantly. "I can take care of myself."

"Under most circumstances, I'm sure you can. But not against a bunch like Gannon's."

The discussion—it hadn't quite descended to the level of an argument yet—had started when Alma once again mentioned her intention to rent a horse and ride back to her grandfather's farm, two days south of Tahlequah. Fargo had said that he didn't think that was a very good idea.

"What do you think I should do?" she asked him now.

"I imagine George Dayton would be happy to give you an escort, along with a couple of other Lighthorsemen."

Alma shook her head. "George is as sweet as a big old puppy, but he's been in love with me since I was fourteen years old, Skye. The way he moons around after me is enough to drive any woman mad."

"All the more reason to think he'd want to protect you."

"I don't *want* his protection. I'll get a fast horse. I can outrun trouble if any happens to come along."

Fargo could see that she was as hardheaded as the day was long. She was normally sweet and shy, but when she made up her mind about something, it was difficult, if not impossible, to sway her from her decision.

That left Fargo with no choice. If she wouldn't let George Dayton take her home, then he would have to do it himself.

He saw that the only way of proving what had happened to Dave Donaldson was to ride over to Devil's Den. True, he would be taking his life into his hands by doing so, at least according to what George had said, but Fargo had confidence in his ability to take care of himself. Unfortunately, if what he suspected was true about Dave taking up with the gang of outlaws, it was too late for Fargo to do anything except discover the truth.

But if Dave was an outlaw now, it was more than likely that he would still be an outlaw in a week or so. Fargo's trip to Devil's Den could wait. He would first take Alma back to her grandfather's farm and then resume his search for Dave Donaldson.

And of course, given the Gannon gang's interest in Alma, it was possible that by riding with her, Fargo would run into them along the way.

All he had to do now was get her to agree to let him accompany her on the trip.

"All right," he said.

"All right what?"

"You can get a horse and ride back to your grandfather's farm."

"Thank you," she said.

"But I'm going with you."

A grin stretched across her face. "Did you expect me to argue with you about that?"

Fargo suddenly wondered if that was what she'd been angling for all along. He didn't think that was entirely the case. He recalled that she had made some remark about renting a horse when they were in Dupree's store. That was well before they had spent the night together.

He chuckled and returned her grin. "If I didn't know better, I'd say you were shameless, Alma Cloudwalker."

She might have made some comment in response to that, but before she could, she looked past him and said in a low voice, "There's George."

Fargo turned toward the door of the dining room and saw George Dayton looking around the room. The Lighthorseman's eyes found them at the table, and he started toward them, carrying his hat in his big, callused hands. He gave Fargo a curt nod as he came up to the table, but favored Alma with a big smile.

"Good morning," he said. "How did you sleep?"

"Very well," she replied, and Fargo was glad to see that she was able to keep any sort of coy look off her face. There was no point in making George any more jealous than he probably already was, now that he had found them together. Fargo wasn't frightened of the tribal policeman, of course, but he didn't see any point in aggravating the situation, either.

Without waiting to be invited, George pulled back one of the empty chairs and sat down at the table. "I was afraid you might have still been disturbed by all the trouble yesterday," he said to Alma. "That's why I thought you might not have slept well."

"I'm sorry about Ben and Asa, of course," she told him. "But I'm just mad at Abel Gannon and his bunch. They have no right to do the things they do."

"We'll get them cleaned out sooner or later," George promised grimly. "You can count on that." He turned to look at Fargo, and said, "My captain would like to speak to you about what happened."

"You were there, too," Fargo pointed out. "You can tell him just as much as I can."

"I wasn't around the day before, when Gannon and his men first jumped Alma."

Fargo inclined his head in an acknowledgment of

George's statement. "That's true enough. I'll talk to your captain."

"Good. I'll take you over to the office." The Lighthorseman spoke to Alma again. "You don't mind waiting here in town for a few days until the boys and I can take you back to Jefferson's place, do you?"

Alma picked up her cup and took a sip of her coffee. "As a matter of fact, Mr. Fargo is going to escort me back to the farm."

George's expression hardened a little. "He is, is he? You agreed to do that, Mr. Fargo?"

"Alma wants to get back as soon as she can. She's worried about her grandfather."

"I'd go now," George said, "but Captain Howell wants us to patrol north of here for the next couple of days. He says Gannon never strikes in the same place twice, so since he was south of town yesterday, he'll probably turn up north of town next."

That made sense if that was really the Gannon gang's habit, and the Lighthorsemen ought to know that better than anyone.

"Are you sure you can't wait, Alma?"

"No, George. Grandfather was having trouble getting around when I left. I really have to make sure he's all right."

George looked like he wanted to continue the argument, but he sighed, evidently knowing that he wasn't going to be able to persuade Alma to change her mind. "All right. But you two be careful. A snake like Gannon is just tricky enough to change the way he's been doing things."

"We'll keep our eyes open," Fargo promised. He gestured at the remains of their breakfast. "We're about finished, but you're welcome to join us . . ."

George got to his feet. "No thanks. I've already eaten. And if you're finished, Mr. Fargo, I'll go ahead and take you over to Cherokee headquarters."

Fargo nodded as he stood up. "That's fine." Turning to Alma, he added, "I shouldn't be long."

"I'll see about getting a horse while you're gone," she said. "They ought to have one I can rent at the same stable where you left your horse."

Fargo and George Dayton left the hotel and walked down the street toward the large building that housed the offices of the Cherokee Lighthorse, as well as the chambers of the council that governed nearly all of the affairs of the Cherokee Nation. George led the Trailsman into one of the offices, where a bull-like roar of "Fargo!" greeted them.

Surprised, Fargo stopped short at the sight of the man who stood up behind the room's desk. The man had the voice of a bull and was built like one, too— short and broad and powerful. He had a mop of grizzled hair that grew long in the back. His face, with its high cheekbones and its blade of a nose, could have been carved out of old saddle leather. He came out from behind the desk, grabbed Fargo's hand, and pumped it with an ironlike grip.

Fargo returned the grip with every bit as much strength and grinned at the older man. "It's good to see you again, Ethan," he said. "When George here mentioned Captain Howell, it never occurred to me that it might be you!"

George grunted. "I reckon you two know each other?"

"Fargo and me tracked down a gang of killers a few years ago, over in Missouri," Howell explained. "Haven't seen him since then. We hear plenty about you, though, Fargo. Even the *Cherokee Advocate* has stories in it from time to time about the famous Trailsman."

"You know that most newspaper reporters only have a nodding acquaintance with the truth, Ethan," Fargo said with a grin. "Don't believe everything you read."

"I don't have to. I seen it for myself, with my own two eyes." Howell waved at a ladder-back chair in front of the desk. "Sit down, Fargo. George tells me you've had a couple of run-ins with Abel Gannon and his bunch."

Fargo reversed the chair and straddled it as Howell sat down behind the desk again. "That's right. They were after a wagon being driven by a girl named Alma Cloudwalker."

Howell nodded. "I know her and her grandfather. Fine folks."

"They didn't get the wagon either time, but the second time they managed to stampede the team. The horses ran off in a gully. Killed themselves and wrecked the wagon."

"That's a damn shame." Howell leaned back in his chair and rubbed his jaw in thought. "You know, somebody ought to go after that bunch of cutthroats and thieves and break it up. Might be a handsome reward for the man who could do that."

George spoke up. "Wait just a minute, Captain. The boys and me are planning to run Gannon into the ground."

"And I'm sure you might do that one of these days, George," Howell said with a nod. "Problem is, you'd be mighty close to the line yourselves if you was to shoot those buzzards. They're all white, and we don't have any jurisdiction over 'em."

"But that's not right!" George burst out. "It's Cherokee people they're preying on! They're vultures, just like you said, Captain."

Howell nodded again. "What's right isn't always the same as what is, George. You've got to learn that to get along in this world."

"The white man's world," George said bitterly.

Howell shrugged. "That's the way it is, all right. But now we've got Fargo here to lend us a hand."

Fargo had already figured out—from the captain's comments—what Howell had in mind. He held up a hand to forestall any more of them. "I didn't come here to sign on with the Cherokee Lighthorse, Ethan."

"Then why did you come here?" Howell asked bluntly.

"As a favor to an old friend." Fargo decided to lay his cards on the table. He knew he could trust Ethan Howell, and he figured the same was true of George Dayton. "I'm looking for a white man named Dave Donaldson. His father, Grady Donaldson, helped me out once. Probably saved my life, in fact."

"What makes this Donaldson fella think his son is here in the Nations?"

"The last time Grady saw Dave was in Fort Smith. Dave was talking about going into business with some men and setting up a freight line between Fort Smith and Tahlequah."

Howell shook his head. "There's no such freight line."

"I know. Dave Donaldson also mentioned a place called Devil's Den."

Howell leaned back and rested his palms on the desk as he stared at Fargo. "That's Gannon's stomping ground," he said.

Fargo nodded. "That's what George told me."

George said, "No white man would have any business over there unless . . ."

"Unless he was an outlaw, too," Fargo finished the statement for him when the Lighthorseman's voice trailed off.

Howell chewed on his lower lip for a moment and then asked, "What are you going to do, Fargo?"

"I thought I'd ride over to Devil's Den and have a look around. I'm not going to tell Grady Donaldson that his son has turned outlaw unless I have proof of it."

"And if you get that proof?"

Fargo looked steadily at Howell and said, "Then I'll have done what I promised Grady I would do. I'll have the truth for him. After that, we're even."

Howell sat forward and clasped his hands together. "What I said about a reward for the man who breaks up the Gannon gang still goes, Fargo. When George told me your name, I sent word to Chief John Ross that you were here. He sent a message back ordering me to do whatever I had to do to get you to go after Gannon."

Fargo shook his head. "I told you, Ethan, I've already got a job."

"Not a paying job, though. Just a favor for an old friend. You'd be doing the same for me, only with the prospect of a hefty reward when you're done. And it isn't like you'd be working at cross-purposes with what you're trying to do for this Grady Donaldson, either."

Fargo had to admit that that was true—he could accomplish what he'd set out to do for Grady while, at the same time, working to put the Gannon gang out of business.

"I'll give it some thought," Fargo promised, "but there's something else I have to do first."

"What's that?"

"I told Alma Cloudwalker I'd take her back to her grandfather's place."

George shifted around behind Fargo and cleared his throat. "I could take Alma home, Captain," he offered, "if you'd take back those orders you gave me earlier."

Howell scowled. "No, I want you and your patrol riding the northern part of the district for the next few days. My gut tells me Gannon's liable to try something up there. Fargo's assignment can wait a couple of days."

"But Captain—"

Howell slashed a hand through the air above the desk. "Enough! You have your orders, George, and I expect you to carry them out. And Fargo, your word is good enough for me. If you say you'll go after Abel Gannon once you've got that girl safely back home, I believe it."

Fargo nodded and came to his feet. "We've got a deal, then." He extended his hand, and Howell took it.

But even as he shook hands with the Lighthorse captain, Fargo felt George Dayton's eyes boring holes in his back. Under other circumstances, George might have been a good friend . . .

But now Fargo figured he had made an enemy instead.

7

By the time Fargo got to the livery stable, Alma had picked out a mount and made arrangements with the liveryman to rent it. The horse was a mostly brown gelding with white stockings and a white blaze on its nose. The liveryman threw a saddle on the gelding and told Alma to return the animal the next time she was in Tahlequah. Evidently, the man was an old friend of her grandfather's.

"Thank you, Sam," Alma told him with a smile.

"Don't worry about it," Sam said. "Jefferson don't need to be stayin' out there by himself. That old codger needs somebody to look after him."

Alma laughed. "I won't tell him you said so."

"Oh, no. He'd get his back up about me callin' him old, and I'd never hear the end of it."

Fargo took care of saddling the Ovaro himself. When he was done, he and Alma led their horses out onto the street. "I'll pick up a few more supplies," he told her, "and then we'll be ready to ride."

"All right. I still have to settle my bill at the hotel, so I'll do that while you're getting the supplies."

Fargo took out a coin and gave it to her. "My hotel bill needs to be paid, too. Appreciate it if you'd take care of that for me."

"Of course," she said as he handed her the coin.

Fargo headed down the street after tying the two horses to the hitching post outside the stable. Since

Dupree's Emporium was the only store in Tahlequah he knew anything about, he decided to get the supplies there. He figured the store would have everything he and Alma would need.

Business was at a lull when Fargo went inside. He didn't see any customers in the aisles between the shelves, nor was anyone waiting at the counter in the rear of the big room. No clerks were in sight, either. The only person behind the counter was Eva Dupree.

She greeted Fargo with a smile. "Good morning. What can I do for you?" The slow, sensuous way she spoke made the question sound like more than it really was.

Or maybe it didn't, Fargo thought, as he took note of the way Eva's eyes played over his buckskin-clad body.

He pretended not to notice, though. He figured he didn't have time for any complications like that. "I need some flour and salt, and a box of forty-four-caliber shells if you have them."

"Of course. How much flour and salt?"

Fargo thought about it for a second and then said, "Two pounds of flour, half a pound of salt."

Eva nodded. "I'll get it right away. Anything else I can do for you?"

Again Fargo thought the words might have more than one meaning. "No, that'll do it." As Eva began to gather the supplies, he looked around the store and added, "You're not very busy this morning."

"It's late enough so that the morning rush is over," she explained. "Things will pick up again later." She put the sacks of flour and salt on the counter and then turned to get the box of cartridges from a high shelf behind the counter.

As she reached up, Fargo caught a glimpse of her neatly turned ankle. Instinctively, his eyes moved up her legs to the swell of her hips. When she turned around, he saw the boldness in her eyes and knew she was aware of his gaze.

"I like this time of the day," she said. "I like to be alone to think about things."

"Where's your husband?" Fargo asked bluntly.

"Not here." Eva waved a hand in a dismissive gesture. "I'm not sure where he is. Simon goes his way, and I go mine."

Fargo drew a deep breath. Eva's flirting was so obvious that she might as well have hiked her skirts and lain down behind the counter. Fargo knew good and well he wasn't going to take her up on her thinly veiled invitation. For one thing, her husband could walk in at any moment, or someone else could. The front doors of the store were unlocked. Surely the emporium wouldn't be without customers all morning.

For another thing, although Eva Dupree was undeniably, even breathtakingly, lovely, Fargo wasn't the sort of man who normally slept with married women. Which was not to say it had never happened, but the circumstances had to be right, and these definitely weren't.

As if to confirm Fargo's thoughts, the front door opened and Simon Dupree came into the store, whistling under his breath. He walked back to the counter and gave Fargo a pleasant nod. "Good morning," he said. Then he turned to his wife and went on, "I took care of that business at the bank."

So she had known where he was, after all, Fargo thought. Not only that, but she probably had also known when to expect him back. He wondered what would have happened if he had made the advances that Eva seemed to want. More than likely, she would have screamed and carried on as if he had attacked her. Fargo's eyes narrowed angrily. He didn't like it when someone toyed with other people's feelings. Eva Dupree, he realized, was like a beautiful, spoiled child who enjoyed pulling the wings off flies.

And she probably regarded men as little more than flies, too.

When he looked at her, she pushed the supplies

across the counter and told him the price. Her voice was now flat and toneless, instead of being smoky and flirtatious. As Fargo paid, Dupree asked, "Are you leaving town, Mr. Fargo?"

"I'm going to take Miss Cloudwalker back to her grandfather's place," Fargo said. There was clearly no secret about the plans he and Alma had made.

Dupree nodded. "I'm glad to hear it. I was a little worried about her riding back down to Jefferson's place by herself, what with Gannon's bunch still on the loose. Someone needs to run them into the ground."

Fargo didn't say anything about accepting the assignment—from Captain Ethan Howell—to do just that. Dupree didn't need to be in on *all* of Fargo's plans.

Fargo picked up the supplies and nodded to the two of them. "So long," he said.

"Good-bye, Mr. Fargo," Dupree replied. Eva said nothing, but when Fargo glanced at her, he saw anger smoldering in her dark eyes, an expression that vanished instantly as her husband turned toward her.

This was one lady who didn't like being rejected, even when she had no intention of carrying out her invitation, Fargo thought, as he left the store.

Alma waited for him with the horses in front of the livery stable. As he walked up to her, carrying the supplies, she pushed back her long black hair and asked, "Do you have everything we need?"

Fargo nodded. "I'm ready if you are," he said.

Alma smiled at him. "I'm ready."

Fargo stowed the provisions and ammunition in his saddlebags, and then swung up onto the Ovaro. Alma mounted her horse with ease, and as Fargo saw the way she sat her saddle, he knew she must have practically grown up on the back of a horse. Her being an experienced rider would make the trip easier.

As they rode out, Fargo thought he felt that eyes were watching them. He glanced around and saw that

Eva Dupree had stepped out of the store and onto the porch. She was too far away for him to make out much about her expression, but he didn't think she looked happy.

He *knew* George Dayton wasn't happy. They passed the Cherokee Lighthorseman as he leaned on a hitch rail. He lifted a hand in a gesture of farewell and called out, "So long, Alma. I'll drop by your grandfather's place next time I'm down that way."

She gave him a smile. "All right, George," she said. "Thank you for all your help."

When they were well past him, Fargo said in a low voice, "He's smitten with you, all right."

"And I feel bad that I don't feel the same way about him." Alma shook her head. "But I just don't."

"You shouldn't feel bad about that," Fargo said. "You're just being honest with yourself."

"That's important to you? Being honest, I mean."

"When it comes down to it," Fargo said, "whether or not he's honest is all any man has."

"That's an awfully narrow way of looking at things. What about love?"

Fargo smiled. "Well, maybe I stated it a mite too strong. Love's important, too. But you can't have love without honesty."

"Perhaps. But are we going to talk philosophy all the way back to my grandfather's farm?"

Fargo grinned now. "Lord, I hope not."

They left Tahlequah behind and headed south.

The day passed uneventfully. Fargo kept a close eye out for any sign of the Gannon gang. The outlaws didn't put in an appearance, though, and he wondered if they had indeed moved up to the area north of Tahlequah to continue their banditry, as Captain Ethan Howell had suspected they might.

Alma was solemn and silent as they passed the spot where the outlaw ambush had cost the lives of two

Lighthorsemen, as well as the horses and her grandfather's wagon. Fargo waited until they were well past the place before he resumed the conversation.

That night, they camped on top of a hill, a short distance off the trail. They made a cold camp, since the weather was warm enough that they didn't have to have a fire. Also, Fargo didn't want to draw any more attention to them than was necessary. Alma didn't complain about the lack of hot food. She was much more interested in making love to Fargo on the blanket they spread out beneath a tree.

After they had sated themselves, they slept well and woke up early the next morning, ready to ride on.

They passed several isolated farms during the day and, a couple of times, encountered wagons on the trail. The men driving the wagons knew Alma and greeted her warmly. They also asked about her grandfather's health. Clearly, Jefferson Cloudwalker was well known in this part of Indian Territory.

Fargo enjoyed Alma's company. She was not only beautiful, but she was intelligent as well. She told him that she had attended the Cherokee Female Academy in Park Hill and graduated from the school with honors. Someday she intended to teach school herself, but not just yet. Fargo got the feeling she didn't intend to pursue that career as long as her grandfather was alive and she had to care for him.

The journey was so pleasant that he hated to see it end, but that afternoon they topped a rise and looked down into a shallow valley through which a creek meandered. A sturdy-looking log cabin sat on a knoll not far from the stream. Smoke rose from its chimney. A barn and a chicken coop were nearby. Beyond them Fargo saw a line of large, raised boxes that he knew had to be Jefferson Cloudwalker's beehives.

Alma reined in and sighed with pleasure at the sight of her home. Then a shadow passed across her face. "I wish I didn't have such bad news for my grandfather."

"Can he replace the wagon and team?" Fargo asked.

Alma shook her head. "I don't see how. The farm doesn't produce much. Most of my grandfather's money comes from selling the honey he collects from the hives."

"Does Simon Dupree buy most of the honey?"

"Yes. Grandfather sells a few kegs to individuals, but most of it goes to Mr. Dupree's store."

Fargo thought about the task he would face once he had delivered Alma safely to her home. It was possible that if he broke up the Gannon gang, he would recover some of the loot stolen by the outlaws. In that case, he would do his best to see that Alma and her grandfather were reimbursed a sufficient amount to replace the wagon and horses. After all, Gannon was to blame for their loss.

They rode on down the gentle slope to the farm. A couple of big yellow dogs came out of the barn and barked at them. The commotion brought an elderly man out of the house. He was stooped, and walked carefully with the aid of a gnarled cane. His hair was snow-white above a dark, sharply planed face. He broke into a grin as he watched Alma dismount.

She ran over to him and threw her arms around him. Fargo noted that she was careful not to hug him too hard—old bones were brittle.

Fargo swung down from the Ovaro. Alma, with her arm around her grandfather's shoulders, brought the old man over to him. "Grandfather, this is my friend Skye Fargo," she said. "Skye, my grandfather Jefferson Cloudwalker."

Fargo shook hands with Cloudwalker, who said, "Ah, the Trailsman. You were at Fort Gibson several years ago, working for the army."

"That's right," Fargo agreed. He was careful not to exert too much strength as he clasped Cloudwalker's bony hand.

"I was a scout for them, farther north on the plains, when the soldiers rode against the Pawnee and the Cheyenne. You don't remember me from Fort Gibson, do you?"

Fargo shook his head. "I'm afraid not."

"I was not so old then. My strength, it is gone from me now. The past two years have been as twenty." Cloudwalker sighed. "The time to meet my ancestors draws closer all the time."

"Grandfather!" Alma exclaimed. "You shouldn't talk like that."

"But it is true," the old man insisted.

"All our days are numbered," Fargo said. "That's why we have to live them the best we can."

Cloudwalker smiled. "You think like an Indian, my friend." He looked at Alma and grew more serious. "Where are the wagon and the horses?"

"Grandfather . . ." Alma swallowed hard. "Grandfather, I have some bad news."

Cloudwalker rested both hands on the head of his cane and pushed himself up until he was standing almost straight. "Tell me," he commanded bluntly.

Alma did so, but clearly it was hard for her to get out the words. The angles of Cloudwalker's face seemed to become even more sharply defined as his features grew taut with anger and strain. When Alma finished the story, he rasped, "Gannon did this?"

"Yes."

"Someone should kill that man. If I were ten years younger . . . even five years . . . I would do it myself."

"Now, Grandfather—" Alma began.

He turned a fierce glare on her. "To you, I am a doddering old man. But I fought my battles and I have my honor. That will not change, no matter how weak my body becomes. This man—" He looked at Fargo. "This man understands what I say."

Fargo nodded. "Yes, I do. And your spirit will ride with me, Cloudwalker, when I seek out the one called Gannon and bring him and his men to justice."

"Skye, what are you talking about?" Alma exclaimed.

Cloudwalker looked intently at Fargo. "You would do this thing?"

"I've given my word to my old friend Ethan Howell that I'll try."

Slowly, Cloudwalker nodded. "Ethan is a good man, devoted to the law. Of course he would try to enlist the aid of the Trailsman."

"You didn't tell me anything about this, Skye," Alma said.

"Didn't see any reason to," Fargo replied. "I promised to bring you home, so I had to do that first, anyway."

"So I was just a chore to you?" As she spoke, Fargo saw the same warrior spirit flare in her eyes that had been so obvious in her grandfather's eyes a few moments earlier. She came by it honestly, he thought, with a silent chuckle.

Cloudwalker reached over to take Fargo's arm and lead him toward the cabin before Fargo had to answer Alma's question. "You will share our table and stay under our roof tonight," he said, his tone leaving no room for argument—not that Fargo intended to argue.

"I'm obliged," Fargo said.

Alma followed them into the cabin, her lovely face still angry.

The atmosphere in the cabin that evening was a bit strained but not too bad. Fargo thought that, for the most part, Alma had gotten over being irritated with him. She was worried, though, and she said as much over the supper she prepared.

"Gannon always has at least a dozen men around him. You're only one man, Skye. How can you do anything when the entire Cherokee Lighthorse brigade has failed?"

"Sometimes one man can reach places an entire army cannot," Cloudwalker said before Fargo could answer.

He nodded. "That's what I'm hoping. I'm going to take a ride up to Devil's Den."

"That is an evil place," Cloudwalker said solemnly.

Fargo grinned across the table at the old man. "Then it's probably the best place to look for evil men."

When the meal was over, Cloudwalker got to his feet and said, "I must check on the hives." He shuffled out of the cabin.

Fargo looked at Alma. "Should I go help him?"

She shook her head without hesitation and said, "No, Grandfather always tends to the hives himself. He won't let anyone else help him, not even me. He says this is the way it has always been and the way it will always be."

"Not always," Fargo said gently.

"I know. But as long as he can manage, I plan to let him carry on as he always has."

"Probably the best thing to do," Fargo said as he got to his feet. "Thanks for supper. It was a fine meal."

She came around the table and put her arms around his neck, smiling at him as she did so. "If you really want to thank me, I can think of another way for you to do it."

Fargo inclined his head toward the door. "Your grandfather is right outside."

"I know. I didn't mean right now. But later . . . I'll come to the barn after Grandfather goes to sleep . . ."

Fargo intended to bunk down in the barn. What Alma proposed sounded mighty nice, he thought, and he suspected that he was likely to take her up on the offer.

For now, though, there was time for a kiss before Cloudwalker came in from checking on his bees.

Fargo brought his mouth down on Alma's and drank in the warm sweetness of her lips. Gentle at first, the kiss quickly became urgent with passion. Fargo was a patient man, but he looked forward to the moment, later in the evening, when Alma would come to the barn to pay him a visit. A blanket spread on a pile of straw made a perfectly fine bed . . .

The sudden crackle of gunfire outside made them jerk apart.

"Grandfather!" Alma gasped.

Fargo spun around and lunged toward the cabin door. By the time he reached it, the Colt was in his hand. He didn't hear any bullets hitting the log walls of the cabin. The shots seemed to be directed elsewhere.

Fargo shouldered the door open, and went into a rolling dive that carried him out of the light that spilled through the doorway. He rose to his feet and darted toward the barn. His keen eyes searched the night for muzzle flashes.

Colt flame bloomed in the darkness, under the trees on the far side of the hives. Fargo ran in that direction and snapped a couple of shots toward the hidden gunmen. Something buzzed past his ear. He didn't know if it was a bullet or an angry bee.

Where was Jefferson Cloudwalker? Fargo looked for him around the hives and spotted a dark shape sprawled on the ground. Grimly, he ran in that direction, zigzagging to make himself a more difficult target. He threw himself to the ground, landing next to the fallen man, and then reached out to grasp his shoulder. Bullets punched through the hive above their heads. Bees swarmed out, furious at being disturbed.

Fargo knew the bees could be dangerous. One sting was an annoyance; a thousand stings were deadly. Working with the little winged creatures, Cloudwalker had probably been stung enough times over the years so that their venom had a lesser effect on him. Fargo didn't have that protection.

Flying lead was even more dangerous, he reminded himself. He wanted to grab Cloudwalker and drag him away from the hives, but he would have to stand up

97

to do that. If he did, the bushwhackers were liable to riddle him.

A fiery pain lanced into the back of his left hand. A second later, he felt a second sting on his neck. The stinging bees couldn't penetrate the tough buckskin, but they could attack all of his exposed skin and would no doubt crawl into his clothes if he stayed here very long.

Suddenly, rifle shots blasted from the direction of the cabin—Alma was giving him a hand, using Fargo's Henry. After three shots, she paused and called out, "Skye, I'll cover you! Get Grandfather out of there!"

Fargo knew he would have to chance it. He holstered his Colt, and as Alma opened fire again, he grabbed Cloudwalker under the old man's arms, and surged to his feet.

Cloudwalker seemed to be unconscious. That proved to be a mixed blessing. He didn't struggle against Fargo, but he was dead weight. Luckily, he didn't weigh much. Fargo hefted the skinny figure over his shoulder and broke into a crouching run toward the cabin.

Another bee stung him before he reached the cabin, but most of the creatures stayed around the hive. A bullet whistled by Fargo's ear. From the door of the cabin, Alma continued her covering fire, aiming at an angle beyond Fargo and her grandfather. Fargo called on all the speed he had and dashed to safety.

Alma slammed the door behind him and dropped the bar across it. The cabin had not been built with this sort of defense in mind, but Fargo had seen enough of it to know that the walls were strong and thick. He was confident that he and Alma could hold the place against an attack, unless they faced an overwhelming force.

"Grandfather . . . ?" she said as Fargo lowered the old man to the floor in front of the fireplace.

Fargo saw Cloudwalker's chest rise and fall. "He's alive," he said curtly. "I can't tell how bad he's hurt."

As a matter of fact, Fargo couldn't see any wounds on the old man's body. It looked like Cloudwalker had simply passed out. Then Fargo spotted the bloody streak in the old man's thick white hair and parted the strands, revealing a raw furrow in the skin above his left ear.

"A bullet creased him, knocked him out. But I reckon he'll be all right." Fargo looked up at Alma and went on, "They'll be coming any minute. Do you have any more guns around here?"

"An old shotgun and a single-shot rifle."

"Get them," Fargo said as he straightened from where he knelt beside Cloudwalker and took the Henry from her. "Make sure they're loaded."

As he glided low toward the window, the glass in the pane shattered. A bullet went on across the room and embedded itself in the heavy mantel over the fireplace. Fargo paused and then blew out the lamp, plunging the cabin into darkness. No point in making it any easier for the bastards, he thought.

He couldn't be sure who was out there, but he suspected the attackers were Abel Gannon and his gang. Maybe Dave Donaldson was among them. Fargo didn't let himself think too much about that. The bushwhackers had called the turn. Now they all had to dance to it.

Fargo wondered, though, why Gannon seemed to have such a grudge against the Cloudwalkers. If that really was the Gannon gang, and if they were responsible for the two attacks on Alma while she was on her way to Tahlequah, this would make three times, in less than a week, that the bunch had come after the Cloudwalkers. If Fargo didn't know better, he would say that there might be something personal about the whole affair, as if Abel Gannon had indeed had some sort of grudge against the family.

He could deal with those questions later, Fargo told himself, as he knelt beside the shattered window, pressing the smooth stock of the repeating rifle to his cheek.

Right now, he had to worry about keeping himself, along with Alma and her grandfather, alive, while there was a whole gang of killers out there who seemed to want them dead.

8

Just as Fargo expected, moments later, he heard the swift rataplan of hoofbeats in the darkness. Riders galloped toward the cabin, their guns flashing. Fargo returned the fire, taking his time as he levered the Henry between shots and placed his bullets carefully. It was too dark to tell if he had hit any of the outlaws, but he thought the rate of their gunfire dropped off, as if a few of them had been knocked out of the fight.

"Skye, what should I do?" Alma asked in a low voice, during a lull in the shooting.

"You've got that scattergun you mentioned?"

"Yes." Her voice seemed steady enough, but Fargo sensed she wouldn't be able to stand up to a lor siege.

The cabin had only one door, but there was a la rear window. "Get over by that back window," Fa told Alma. "Stay as low as you can. But if you anybody, cut loose with one barrel."

"Not both barrels?"

Fargo smiled grimly. "Save the second barrel i there's two of them."

"Oh. That makes sense."

He heard the shuffle of her feet as she scuttl to the back window. Outside, the raiders had off their attack on the cabin. Fargo didn't be a second that they were really gone, though. just pulled back to regroup.

Sure enough, a few moments later the riders again burst out of the trees on the far side of the beehives. This time several of them carried torches. Some of them flung the torches under the hives. Fargo grimaced when he saw that, but there was nothing he could do about it. Jefferson Cloudwalker's handiwork was about to be destroyed.

But the bees themselves would be all right. The smoke from the torches would make them scatter. Cloudwalker and Alma could rebuild the hives later, and the bees would return.

Assuming, of course, that they lived through this night.

More of the torch-wielding marauders raced toward the cabin. Fargo picked off one of them and felt a surge of satisfaction when he saw the man go cartwheeling out of the saddle. But then he had to duck as the other members of the gang concentrated a fierce volley of shots on the front window, where he was crouching.

He heard a couple of thuds above his head and knew that torches had been thrown onto the roof. The fire would catch and spread quickly. Fargo, Alma, and Cloudwalker had a choice: they could stay in here and die from smoke and flames, or they could go out and be shot down like dogs.

But maybe there was a third option. Fargo said, "Alma, check the back window! You see anybody?"

"No," she replied. Smoke had already begun to curl down into the room from the burning roof. "Skye, what are we going to do?"

He started to turn away from the front window, but he paused for a second as he caught sight of one of the outlaws, who had sat his horse near the blazing hives. In the garish red light of the flames, the man seemed huge, almost big enough to dwarf the massive horse he rode. His shoulders, chest, and belly stretched the flannel shirt he wore. He had a bristling

black beard that came halfway down his chest, and a high-crowned black hat was shoved down on a thatch of black hair. He sat his horse like a king surveying a battlefield where he had just led his army to victory.

Fargo's gut told him he was looking at Abel Gannon.

He would have tried a quick shot, but Gannon suddenly spun his horse around and lunged out of the light, as if he had sensed the danger that threatened him. Fargo lowered the Henry.

"Get out the back," he told Alma. "Then cover me while I get your grandfather."

He knew, from experience, how lithe and agile she was. Carrying the shotgun, she scrambled over the windowsill and dropped to the ground outside. Fargo picked up Jefferson Cloudwalker and draped the old man over his left shoulder. He carried the Henry in his right hand. The shooting had started again, and slugs whistled eerily around the room as he hurried to the window.

Fargo's legs were long enough to allow him to step over the sill. Alma was right there, saying, "Let me help you."

Fargo snapped, "Behind you," as a shape loomed out of the darkness. Alma whirled around and brought up the Greener. It roared as she touched off one of the barrels, just as Fargo had told her to do. The man who had run at them didn't even have time to cry out, as the charge of buckshot slammed him backward into hell.

Half falling, Fargo caught himself and kept from dropping Cloudwalker. The old man let out a groan and stirred slightly. He was starting to regain consciousness. This wasn't a very good time for that, Fargo thought, but there was nothing he could do about it. He gave a shrill whistle and then repeated the sound.

Just as he hoped, the Ovaro smashed through the

flimsy gate to the barn stall where Fargo had put him earlier. The big black-and-white stallion burst out of the barn and raced toward his master.

Over the shots and the crackle of the flames and the thudding of hoofbeats, Fargo heard a deep voice bellow, "Around back! Around back, you lunkheads! You're too damn slow!"

That would be the voice of Abel Gannon, roaring orders. Fargo figured the outlaws would be risking their own lives if they didn't obey Gannon's warning.

Fargo caught the Ovaro's mane as the horse came up to him. "Get on," he said to Alma.

There was no time for a saddle. She climbed on to ride bareback, throwing her leg over the stallion's back. Fargo lifted her grandfather toward her. She caught hold of him and pulled him up in front of her.

"Hang on tight," Fargo told her. "Ride as hard as you can away from here."

"What about you, Skye?" she asked desperately.

"I'll get that horse you brought from Tahlequah." Precious seconds were slipping away. "Go!" he urged her.

The Ovaro responded to Fargo's command as much as he did to the banging of Alma's heels against his flanks. Breaking into a run, the horse streaked off smoothly into the darkness.

Fargo ran for the barn. Riders came around the corner of the burning cabin as he did so. Bullets kicked up dust around his feet and plucked at the sleeve of his shirt. He tossed the rifle from his right hand to his left, and then the right swooped down to palm out the Colt. He emptied it on the raiders, driving them back for a moment and giving him a chance to duck into the barn.

The other horse was spooked by all of the uproar. It danced around as much as it could in the stall and whinnied shrilly as Fargo approached. He bit back a curse. He didn't have time to calm down the animal. He would just have to do the best he could.

He yanked the stall gate open and grabbed for the horse's mane, pulling down hard to bring it under control. The horse fought him, but Fargo knew what he was doing. In a matter of moments, he was on the horse's back, kicking it into a run toward the front of the barn.

The Henry still had several shots in it. Fargo triggered all of them as he slammed out of the barn at a gallop. He swung the rifle from side to side as he levered the rounds into the chamber and pulled the trigger. Lead sprayed from the muzzle.

More bullets zipped around his head like those angry bees had done earlier. The outlaws bulked in a silhouette against the leaping flames that consumed the cabin. Fargo didn't know if he had hit any of them. All he knew was that he broke through them as they tried to close in on him. He rode through a cloud of smoke that billowed from the cabin. Coughing, he emerged from the acrid black cloud and breathed deeply in the cool night air. That soothed his lungs and cleared his head as he galloped through the darkness.

The horse ran gamely enough, but it lacked the speed and stamina of the Ovaro. Fargo knew he couldn't push it for very long at this pace. He had to put as much distance as he could, though, between himself and any pursuit by the outlaws. He listened, trying to hear hoofbeats behind him as he took some cartridges from his pocket and reloaded the Henry while he rode.

Most of his extra ammunition was back there on the Cloudwalker farm. He knew the odds were against him. But he wasn't the sort of man to give up.

He wondered where Alma and her grandfather were.

A glance back showed him that the sky was red above the burning cabin and the hives. Jefferson Cloudwalker didn't have any close neighbors, Alma had said, but that hellish glow could be seen for a long way. Some of the other Cherokee who lived in the area would probably ride over to see what was going on. Gannon and his men wouldn't hang around for too long. If Alma kept moving, she stood a good chance of getting away with the old man.

Fargo intended to do the same thing.

When the horse began to falter a short time later, Fargo eased up on the prodding and let the animal slow to a walk and then finally come to a stop. The Trailsman slid down from the horse's back and stood there, hatless, with his rifle held firmly in his hands, and his keen ears listening for any sounds of the outlaws giving chase.

He didn't hear anything, but that didn't mean they weren't back there somewhere, closing in on him slowly but surely. The chances were that they knew this part of the country quite a bit better than he did.

Fargo looked up at the sky, studying the panoply of lights against a sable backdrop. He could tell, from the position of certain stars, where he was and what time it was. He realized that he had ridden north from the Cloudwalker farm. He wasn't sure, but he thought Alma and her grandfather had come in this direction, too.

He had wanted to pay a visit to Devil's Den, Fargo thought, with a wry smile. Well, now he was at least going generally in the right direction.

But even if the outlaws didn't pursue him, they would be coming this way, too. It wasn't safe to just stand here and wait.

Fargo got moving, walking at first. The horse followed. After a while he rode, and that was the pattern he held to all night, switching back and forth between riding and walking so that the horse wouldn't get too tired. As for himself, he couldn't worry about how tired he was. He had to ignore his weariness and keep moving.

The night passed slowly, but as the sun came up, Fargo found himself in familiar territory.

Off to his left was a long, open field. Beyond it, perhaps a quarter of a mile away, lay the trail that ran from Fort Smith to Tahlequah. This was near the spot where the runaway wagon had gone into the gully, nearly taking Alma Cloudwalker with it. Fargo heeled the horse into a walk and crossed the field.

He was a couple of hundred yards east of the wreck. The gully twisted and turned so that he couldn't see the wagon or the bodies of the horses. As he came up to the declivity, though, he spotted something interesting down below. A scrubby tree extended its branches over the surface of the creek that flowed at the bottom of the gully. One of the kegs of honey that had come from the wagon had floated downstream and gotten caught in those branches, and surprisingly, it seemed to be unbroken.

A faint smile plucked at Fargo's lips. One keg of honey wouldn't mean that much, one way or the other, to Alma and her grandfather, but he decided to recover it, anyway. Maybe getting it back would make them feel better about their situation.

During the night, Fargo had pulled some of the long strands of fringe off his buckskins and knotted them together to fashion a makeshift hackamore. Now he tied the harness to a bush so that the gelding wouldn't stray. Before climbing down into the gully, he spent a long moment studying his back trail. He didn't see anyone moving, or any dust in the air, or any other sign of the Gannon gang. He could afford to pause for a few minutes. The horse could use the rest, anyway.

Fargo worked his way down the slope into the gully. When he reached the bottom, he held onto the thin trunk of a sapling for balance, and leaned out over the creek to reach for the keg with his other hand. He was able to work it toward him, and after a few minutes he got a good hold on it and pulled it out of the water.

As soon as he picked it up, he knew something was wrong.

Honey was thick, and flowed slowly. Anyone who tapped a barrel or keg of honey had to be patient while the sweet, sticky stuff ran out.

But whatever was inside this keg was *sloshing* around. It was a much thinner liquid than honey should be.

Fargo studied the keg, thinking that maybe it had cracked open somewhere and creek water had diluted the contents. But he saw that it was intact. Curiosity got the better of him. He reached down and pulled the Arkansas Toothpick from the sheath on his leg. It took only a moment of working with the heavy blade to pry off the keg's lid.

The sharp tang of raw whiskey immediately assailed Fargo's nostrils.

Whiskey! The stuff was forbidden here in the Nations—which meant there was a potential profit to be made by those who smuggled it in, or brewed it themselves.

Fargo's mind worked rapidly. If the back of Jefferson Cloudwalker's wagon had been filled with kegs of whiskey, rather than kegs of honey, it would have been worth a small fortune. That was reason enough right there for a gang of outlaws, such as the one led by Abel Gannon, to be after it. Even if some of the kegs had really contained honey, as seemed likely, the load would still be worth a lot.

The only thing wrong with that whole theory was that it meant Cloudwalker was brewing illegal liquor. That would make him a criminal. And Fargo didn't see how Alma couldn't have known about it.

Putting aside, for the moment, the question of Alma's possible involvement, Fargo's mind leaped ahead. The cargo had been bound for Simon Dupree's store in Tahlequah. Dupree must have known that it included whiskey. Fargo could imagine an entire whiskey ring, with Jefferson Cloudwalker as the supplier and Dupree as the distributor. Everything he had seen so far indicated that Gannon wanted to horn in on that.

Fargo frowned as he considered what he should do next. He liked a drink as much as the next man and didn't object, in principle, to whiskey. But to produce, sell, or even possess the stuff here in Indian Territory was against the law, and by and large, Fargo was a law-abiding man. Part of his brain said that he ought to go back to Tahlequah and tell Captain Ethan Howell what was going on. The Cherokee Lighthorse could break up the ring and put Cloudwalker out of business.

But that would mean the old man would probably wind up in jail, and Alma might, too. Fargo would hate for that to happen.

Not only that, but he still had the problem of Dave Donaldson to deal with. To find out the truth about Dave, he had to break up Gannon's gang, and it seemed to Fargo that Gannon and the other outlaws were a greater threat to the Cherokee people than Jefferson Cloudwalker's whiskey was. Maybe what he needed to do was to have a talk with Cloudwalker and warn the old man to stop cooking up whiskey. He felt certain that once Cloudwalker knew someone was on to what he was doing, he would cease rather than risk getting Alma in trouble with the law.

That was what Fargo hoped, anyway.

In the meantime, he had this keg of whiskey in his hands, and he had to do something with it. He took a taste of it and licked his lips appreciatively. It was pretty good stuff.

"Damn shame," Fargo said aloud as he upended the keg and poured the contents into the creek.

"Ain't it though?" said a voice behind him.

Fargo froze with the keg still in his hands. He had brought the Henry rifle down into the gully with him, but it was leaning against a tree, and he estimated it would take him a couple of seconds to drop the keg, whirl around, and snatch up the rifle. In that much time, a man who was good with a gun could put several rounds through him.

His instincts told him the man behind him probably had a gun pointed at him and knew how to use it. There was something vaguely familiar about the voice, but Fargo couldn't place it right away.

"Toss that keg in the creek, too," the man went on. "Now that it's empty, it's not any good to anybody."

Fargo hesitated. He might not have the rifle in his hands, but he still held something that could be used as a weapon. But the man who had the drop on him had to know that, too. That was why he had told Fargo to throw the keg away.

If Fargo was going to use it, he had to be quick—to think was to act. The Trailsman lifted the keg over his head as if he were about to toss it into the creek, as he had been ordered to do, but then he flung himself to the side and twisted in midair. He threw the keg as hard as he could at the man who had come up behind him.

Fargo's instincts had taken over, and luckily, they were correct. His twisting dive took him out of the line of fire. The man's gun blasted, but the bullet screamed harmlessly through the air and plunged into the creek. The man's reflexes had forced him to duck just as he fired. Even so, the keg struck him on the shoulder and knocked him back a step.

Fargo rolled over and rose to his feet as the gunman caught his balance and tried to bring the barrel of the gun back in line. It was too late. Fargo lunged forward and left his feet, making a flying tackle. He batted the gun aside just before he crashed into the man. The revolver roared again as both men fell.

In that brief instant before the collision, Fargo had gotten a good look at the man. He recognized the dusty black suit, the black hat, the close-cropped fair hair, the square chin.

Fargo had no idea what Matt Kenton was doing

here in Indian Territory, but the gunman was definitely the gambler from Fort Smith. Landing on top of him, Fargo drove a knee into Kenton's belly and smashed a fist against his jaw. Kenton went limp, and Fargo thought he looked unconscious.

But the gambler was just shamming. He bucked up suddenly from the ground and threw Fargo to the side. Fargo managed to grab Kenton's wrist as he fell. He slammed Kenton's gun hand against the ground, knocking the pistol loose from his grip.

Kenton yelled a profanity and lunged after Fargo, reaching out to fasten a hand around the Trailsman's throat. His fingers clamped down like iron and cut off Fargo's air. Fargo tried to tear free from Kenton's grip but failed.

The faces of the two men were now only inches apart. Kenton's features were twisted in a grimace of anger and hate. He got his other hand on Fargo's neck and squeezed harder. A red haze began to form in front of Fargo's eyes. The world blurred.

Cupping both hands, Fargo slammed them against Kenton's ears. Kenton howled in pain and jerked back. His fingers slipped off Fargo's throat. Fargo got a hand on Kenton's shoulder and shoved hard, thrusting him away. That literally gave Fargo some breathing room. He dragged air down his sore windpipe and into his starving lungs, as he rolled over, struggled to his hands and knees, and then came to his feet.

He was exhausted, having made the long flight from Jefferson Cloudwalker's farm with no sleep and no real rest. Kenton was much fresher, and for a man who spent most of his time inside a saloon, playing cards, he was strong and a good brawler. He charged Fargo now, swinging a powerful punch that the Trailsman barely avoided.

Fargo backed off, drawing Kenton into another bull-like rush. A second earlier, Fargo had spotted the empty keg on the ground. Now, as Kenton lunged at him, he kicked the keg into the gambler's path. Kenton let out a startled yell as he tripped over it and fell forward, out of control. Fargo swung a fist and timed the punch perfectly. Kenton ran right into the blow and dropped as if he had been hit with a sledge.

This time, he really was out cold. Fargo saw that and turned to look for the gun Kenton had dropped at the beginning of the fight. He spotted the six-shooter lying on the ground and reached for it, but before his fingers could close around the grip, a rifle cracked and a slug smacked into the ground, only a few inches away. Fargo jerked his hand back reflexively.

"Next one goes right through your head, you son of a bitch!"

This shouted threat came from the top of the bank. Fargo looked up from the bottom of the gully and saw a man standing there, silhouetted against the morning sun. He had a little trouble making out the rifleman's features, but he didn't think the man was anybody he had ever seen before.

"You're the most annoying fella I ever did see," the man called down. "And you turn up in the damnedest places. Stay right there."

The man half-slid, half-walked, down into the gully. Fargo watched for a chance to jump him, but the rifle stayed steady on him the whole way down. When the man came closer, he said, "Back away from that gun, Fargo. I don't trust you."

The man was tall, lean, and rawboned. He had a lantern jaw and a tangle of lank, fair hair under a battered old hat. The rifle he carried was a Henry, like Fargo's, and he looked like he knew how to use it.

Fargo had been right about one thing: he had never seen this man before.

But the man knew him. He had called Fargo by name.

Fargo put the man's age in the early twenties. He ventured a guess about the man, even though he didn't really fit the right description. "Dave? Dave Donaldson?" he said.

"What?" The man frowned for a second in confusion, before understanding dawned on him. "Hell, no, I'm not Dave!" he declared. "Dave's not here. My name's Barker."

Fargo caught his breath. *Barker.* The man who had tried to kill him on the road between Dardenelle and Fort Smith. First Kenton and now Barker. Everyone seemed to be converging on Indian Territory, though for what reason, Fargo couldn't have said.

"Kenton was right about you," Barker went on. "You're too damn dangerous to have you pokin' around in our business. That's why he sent word for me to pick you up on the road to Fort Smith and see that you never got there."

"The problem was that the man you recruited to help you wasn't very good at what he was trying to do," Fargo said. As long as Barker was talking, he wasn't pulling the trigger on that rifle. Fargo hoped that the man would reveal some more about what was going on here, too.

"Yeah, that bastard was careless. He deserved to wind up dead." Barker's lip twisted in a snarl. "You do, too, but I reckon I'll wait and see what Abel wants to do with you."

So Barker, Kenton, and Abel Gannon were all connected somehow. Fargo was starting to see things more clearly now, but it was all still pretty confusing.

As he regained consciousness, Matt Kenton rolled onto his side and let out a groan. A moment later he lifted his head and then pushed himself into a sitting position. He lifted a hand to his jaw and worked it back and forth. Then he spat a blob of bloody spittle onto the ground.

"Damn well about time you got here," he growled as he looked up at Barker.

"Yeah, well, after we spotted Fargo comin' down

here into this gully, you told me to work around that way while you went around the other way. My way was longer. Anyway, we got the bastard. Now what do we do with him?"

Kenton didn't answer the question. Instead, he looked at Fargo and asked one of his own: "What the hell did you hit me with?"

Fargo managed a bleak smile. "My fist."

The gambler spat again. "Felt like a mule kicked me. If I didn't already have plenty of reasons to want you dead, I've got one now, mister. Nobody hits me like that and gets away with it, not even the high and mighty Trailsman."

"You want me to kill him, Matt?" Barker lifted the rifle, his angular face betraying his eagerness to shed blood.

Kenton climbed laboriously to his feet. "No, not yet. I'd be perfectly happy to see him bleeding to death, but I reckon we'd better wait and find out what Abel wants us to do with him."

"Yeah, that's kinda what I thought," Barker agreed, although a moment earlier, he had seemed willing enough to murder Fargo. "For one thing, we don't know what happened to the old man and the girl."

Fargo tried not to show his reaction to this statement, but he was happy to hear what Barker had just said. It meant that Alma and her grandfather weren't prisoners of these two, anyway. Fargo still hoped that they had gotten away cleanly from the burning cabin.

Of course, it was still possible that Gannon and the rest of the gang had caught up to them.

Kenton picked up his gun and hat. "Let's get out of this damn gully," he said gratingly. "There's no air down here. I can't breathe."

With two guns covering him, Fargo had no choice, for the moment, except to cooperate. He climbed out of the gully and walked over to the horse that had come from the livery stable in Tahlequah. Kenton kept his pistol trained on Fargo while Barker went to fetch the other two horses.

Just as Barker came back with the mounts, the sound of drumming hoofbeats drifted through the air. Kenton looked to the south and pointed. "A bunch of riders coming," he said. "That'll be Abel and the boys." His grin became malicious as he looked at Fargo, and said, "I may be a gambler, but right now I wouldn't take any bets on you staying alive much longer, mister."

Fargo liked to gamble, too, he thought, but under the circumstances, that was one wager he wouldn't have taken, either. He gazed toward the approaching riders and the black-bearded giant who led them.

9

When Gannon and his men saw that Kenton and Barker had a prisoner with them, they increased their pace and galloped across the field. As Gannon recognized Fargo, a bloodthirsty grin spread across his face. His teeth gleamed within the tangle of his thick black beard. With a shout, he reined in as he and his followers reached the three men at the edge of the gully. Leaning forward in the saddle, the giant outlaw said, "Well, I declare. You boys caught him."

"That's right," Kenton said. "Now what do we do with him?"

"Kill him?" Barker suggested, an eager grin on his face.

Gannon tugged on his long black beard and frowned in thought. "That might be the smart thing to do, all right," he said. "But from what I hear, he's friends with that Lighthorse captain in Tahlequah. Could be Fargo might come in handy if we needed to make a trade of some sort."

Fargo's reaction to that was twofold. He was glad Gannon was making noises like he didn't intend to murder the prisoner out of hand. But at the same time, Fargo had to wonder how Gannon knew there was a connection between him and Ethan Howell. This whole affair was getting more tangled all the time.

Quickly, he scanned the faces of the men with Gannon. His gaze lingered on one of them. The man was

116

big, with broad shoulders and a round face. Curly brown hair showed under his hat. That man fit the description Fargo had of Dave Donaldson. Fargo even thought he saw a family resemblance to Grady Donaldson in the outlaw's features. He suspected he was looking at the reason that he had come to Indian Territory in the first place.

Right now, though, that didn't matter. Fargo had to play for time. He said, "You ought to keep me alive for more reasons than that, Gannon."

The boss of the gang glared at him. "Yeah? Why don't you tell me what they are, Fargo?"

"I know where the old man and the girl were heading." That was a lie—Fargo didn't know where Alma and her grandfather were. But he hoped he could use the dodge to keep Gannon from killing him.

The black-bearded giant laughed. "Why do I need to know that? We burned out the old Indian and busted up the stills he had hidden back in the woods. He's no competition for us anymore. If these damn redskins around here want to get drunk, they'll have to do it on the hooch we bring in from Arkansas."

"I figured you were out to take over the whiskey running around here," Fargo said.

"Hell of a lot more money in that than in robbing a bunch of dirt-grubbin' farmers," Gannon said as he spat.

"You've been planning this for a while, haven't you? You even had Kenton working for you in Fort Smith, steering men to you who wanted to make a quick, dirty dollar." Fargo pointed. "Men like Dave Donaldson there."

"Hey!" Dave exclaimed. "You don't know anything about it, mister!"

Kenton chuckled. "Dave joined up because he was in the hole to me for a lot of money. This was his way of recouping his losses."

"But when his father showed up in Fort Smith looking for him and then got in touch with me, you didn't want me riding over here into Indian Territory to search for him. That's why you sent Barker out to ambush me."

"You've got most of it figured out," Kenton replied with a nod. "Lydia let it slip that Donaldson sent a letter to you. The famous Trailsman." The gambler's mouth twisted. "Well, you sure raised hell, all right, just like we thought you might."

"And you still ain't told me why I ought to keep you alive," Gannon put in.

"Because one time I saved Ethan Howell's life." That wasn't a lie. "If the Cherokee Lighthorse closes in on you, you can use me as a hostage."

Gannon snorted. "That's what I just said a minute ago! Damn, you talk in circles, Fargo. Anyway, those redskin lawmen ain't been able to catch us so far. What makes you think they will now?"

"Because Alma Cloudwalker and her grandfather will tell them where to find you."

"They already know Devil's Den is our stomping ground." Gannon slowly drew his pistol—a long-barreled Remington. "The more I think on it, the more it looks to me like I ought to put a bullet through your head right here and now, Fargo. That's likely to save us all some trouble later on."

Fargo tensed. All he could do, if Gannon raised that gun, was to try to throw himself out of the way of the bullet. The gully was still close behind him. If he could make it down into that brush-choked slash in the earth, he might stand a chance of getting away. A small one, true, but any chance was better than none.

"Wait!" Dave Donaldson croaked in a strained voice.

Gannon glanced angrily at him. "What the hell is it now, boy? You takin' up for this son of a bitch just because him and your old pa are friends?"

"No, but you were right before, Abel," Dave said. "Just because the Cherokees haven't caught up with us before doesn't mean they won't now. If the girl and the old man made it back to Tahlequah, they probably told Captain Howell where we are. What if Howell and his men fog it over to Devil's Den as fast as they can and get there before us? Then having Fargo as a hostage could be useful."

Gannon frowned, and the pistol stayed where it was—by his leg. "Yeah, I reckon that could be so."

Fargo didn't know whether to be grateful to Dave Donaldson or not. By speaking up, the young man had perhaps persuaded Gannon not to kill him right away. On the other hand, if Dave hadn't gotten mixed up with these outlaws in the first place, Fargo wouldn't even be here now.

Of course, that meant he wouldn't have been on hand to help save Alma and her grandfather when the outlaws raided the Cloudwalker farm.

Fargo shoved these thoughts aside. He couldn't change the past. Nobody could. All he could do was try to make the best of the present.

Gannon jammed his gun back in its holster. "All right, get on your horse," he said to Fargo. "I'll take a chance on keepin' you alive . . . for now. But every step of the way between here and Devil's Den, there'll be guns pointed at you. If you try anything, the boys will shoot, and shoot to kill."

"I'm not sure this is a good idea, Abel," Matt Kenton said.

"Yeah, well, you ain't the boss of this gang. I am."

Kenton shrugged. He had to have known that challenging Gannon didn't stand much of a chance of succeeding, and he wasn't going to push the issue.

Fargo climbed onto the gelding. The outlaws closed in around him, so that it would take a miracle for him to get away—and miracles were in short supply in Indian Territory, Fargo thought.

But he was going to get what he had wanted—he was on his way to Devil's Den.

The gang rode all day, following dim trails that took them away from farms and other signs of habitation.

By nightfall, they came within sight of the rugged, thickly wooded foothills where their hideout was located.

Fargo had dozed off occasionally while he was riding. The exhaustion that gripped him was too strong to be denied. It grew even worse as darkness settled in, but the outlaws pushed on, anyway. For the second night in a row, Fargo found himself riding rather than sleeping.

He drew deeply on the reserves of his strength. His naturally hardy constitution, and the strenuous life he had led, enabled him to keep going without collapsing. Even the Trailsman had his limits, though, and if the trek lasted much longer, he might find out what they were.

Sometime during the night, Dave Donaldson edged his horse up alongside Fargo's and said quietly, "You and my father are really friends?"

Fargo nodded. "He saved my life a few years ago, out at the stage station he ran in New Mexico Territory. That was after you and your mother had gone back east to live."

"He told you about that, huh?"

"That's right."

"Probably said that he hated my ma for what she did," Dave said bitterly.

"No, not at all." Fargo kept his tone calm and reasonable, sensing that the young man beside him had been caught in a situation in which he didn't really know what to think or do. "He told me that he didn't blame your mother. I think he always loved her, even after she left."

"Not enough to give up that job with Butterfield, though."

"I'm sure he felt like he had a duty to the stage line. He couldn't just abandon the station."

"Maybe not. But he could have told them to find somebody else to run it. Instead, he stayed there, and now he has even more responsibilities."

"A man has to do what he thinks is right," Fargo said. "When it comes down to it, he's the only one who can make that decision."

"Well, sometimes he makes the wrong decision."

"Sometimes he does," Fargo agreed. There was no arguing with that.

They rode along in silence for a while, but finally Dave said, "Do you know Lydia Mallory, back in Fort Smith?"

"I met her." Fargo left out any mention of what had happened between them.

"Is she . . . is she all right?"

"She seemed to be. She's worried about you, though."

Dave sighed. "I should've asked her to marry me. I shouldn't have worried about her working in a saloon or . . . or anything else about her."

"Maybe you should have," Fargo said, remembering that Lydia had hinted that she would have accepted such a proposal from the young man. If they had gotten hitched, they probably would have stayed in Fort Smith and Dave would never have gotten mixed up with these outlaws.

"She told you about that freight line business?"

"Yep."

Dave gave a short, humorless laugh. "That was just the story Kenton told me to tell people, to explain why I came over into the Nations. There never was a freight line."

"I sort of figured that out," Fargo said dryly.

"He said I could make a lot of money and that he'd forget about what I owed him." Dave looked around at the other riders and lowered his voice even more. "Some of these other boys got mixed up with Abel the same way. We're not really badmen, Fargo, not the way you think."

"Were you there when the gang raided the Cloud-walker place?"

"Yeah, but—" Dave stopped his protest and shook

his head. "Don't reckon I blame you for thinking the way you do about me," he muttered.

What Fargo was really thinking was that under the right circumstances, he might be able to turn Dave Donaldson from an enemy into an ally. Dave might balk again if Gannon started to kill the Trailsman. Bringing the youngster over to his side was a slim hope, but as long as he was alive, Fargo wasn't going to give up.

At last, not long before dawn, Gannon called a halt. It was simply too dark to proceed, especially since the faint trail the gang had been following had led them into a tangle of thickets and ridges and hollows. They needed to wait for sunrise so that they could see where they were going.

Still facing several guns, Fargo dismounted, sat down, and propped his back against a tree trunk. He closed his eyes and instantly fell asleep. It seemed that he had barely dozed off, though, when someone kicked his boot, and a harsh voice said, "Wake up."

Fargo opened his eyes, looked up, and saw Gannon looming over him in the gray light of dawn. He glanced around and saw the other men stirring, getting ready to ride. Fargo noticed that Matt Kenton and Barker weren't with them. The two of them must have split off from the gang earlier in the night, when Fargo wasn't aware of it. He supposed they had headed back to Fort Smith to continue their efforts on behalf of the gang there. Gannon had said that he planned to smuggle in whiskey from Arkansas. Fargo suspected that Kenton and Barker were in charge of that part of the operation. They had probably been over here in the Nations conferring with Gannon when they got roped into helping him search for Fargo after the attack on the Cloudwalker farm.

"Get up," Gannon growled. "Won't take us long to get to the hideout now that it's light."

Stifling a groan, Fargo climbed wearily to his feet. Gannon backed off, covering him with the Remington.

Fargo scrubbed a hand over his face and then shook his head, clearing out some of the cobwebs from his brain. His stomach clenched. He'd had a few pieces of jerky to gnaw on since being captured by the outlaws, but he was still ravenously hungry.

"Get a move on," Gannon ordered. He jerked the barrel of the revolver toward the horses to emphasize the command.

Fargo let himself stumble a little as he walked over to the gelding. To tell the truth, he wasn't quite as tired as he pretended to be. But it couldn't hurt at all to let the outlaws think he was completely worn out. If he got a chance to make a break, he could take them by surprise even more if they didn't believe him to be capable of fast action.

Within a few minutes, the group rode northward again, through terrain that steadily grew more rugged. The trail narrowed until the riders had to take it single file. Gannon led the way. The man directly behind Fargo rode with a pistol trained on the Trailsman's back. Fargo thought about turning the gelding to the side and striking out into the brush, but he discarded the idea as he realized that the tangle was too thick for that to ever work. The horse would have to move so slowly that the gunman behind Fargo would have time to empty the revolver into him before he went ten feet.

Like it or not, he had no choice but to continue on with the gang to their hideout.

They rode across a ridge—covered with tall pines— that blocked the light of the rising sun. When they reached the far side of the ridge, the ground dropped sharply into a deep depression in the earth. Farther east in the Ozarks, people called such a place a "holler"—a corruption of the word *hollow*.

As Fargo rode down the slope, he saw a log cabin that was located at the bottom of the depression. It was difficult to notice at first glance because of all the trees and brush around it. The structure blended into its surroundings so well that a second look was required to distinguish it. Even then, Fargo might not have noticed it if it weren't for the plume of smoke curling up from the stone chimney into the morning sky.

Abel Gannon shifted around in the saddle and looked at Fargo. "This is it, Trailsman," he announced. "Devil's Den."

"Doesn't look very hospitable," Fargo said.

Gannon grinned. "Maybe not, but it's the last place you're likely to ever see."

Fargo said nothing in response. He wasn't going to allow Gannon to get to him, to prey on his mind. Fargo's body was tired, but his spirits were still strong.

He looked around the hollow. No sign of Captain Howell, George Dayton, and the rest of the Cherokee Lighthorsemen. He had hoped, against hope, that Alma and her grandfather had carried the news of the raid to Tahlequah, and that the tribal police would have set up an ambush here at the outlaws' hideout. He had known all along, though, how slim the chances were that such a thing had happened. So he wasn't surprised.

The door of the cabin opened as the group of riders approached. A figure stepped out to greet them, and this time Fargo *was* surprised. Eva Dupree stood there, her hand lifted to shade her eyes from the morning sun. She wore a divided riding skirt and a dark blue blouse that clung to the thrust of her breasts. A gunbelt with a holstered Colt was strapped around her shapely hips.

"What in blazes does this mean?" Fargo asked himself. He had figured out that Jefferson Cloudwalker and Simon Dupree must be partners in the illegal whiskey business, and yet here was Dupree's wife, evidently waiting for the men who were trying to take over that operation.

This puzzle was cleared up as Gannon swung down from the saddle, hurried over to Eva, and swept her up in his arms. She was a substantial woman, but she looked almost like a child as the giant outlaw embraced her. Gannon kissed her, and she returned the kiss with considerable ardor.

Well, Fargo thought, he had suspected that Eva Dupree was none too faithful to her husband. Clearly, she was not only cheating on Dupree but she had also double-crossed him where his business was concerned, throwing in with the Gannon gang. She had probably alerted them to the fact that Alma was bringing a wagonload of whiskey to Tahlequah, and she was also the most likely source of Gannon's knowledge that Fargo and Ethan Howell were old friends. At first, the situation had seemed murky to Fargo, but now everything had been resolved into a clear picture in his mind.

Except, he thought, for the extent of Alma's involvement in the whiskey business. She was still a bit of an unknown quantity. But he could figure that out later, Fargo told himself, assuming that he lived through the whole mess.

Gannon set Eva back on the ground but kept his tree-trunk arms around her waist. "I was hopin' you'd be waitin' for us," he said with a grin.

She looked at Fargo and frowned worriedly. "That's Skye Fargo. What's he doing here?"

Gannon's grin turned into a scowl as he turned his head to look at Fargo. "He turned up at Cloudwalker's place, like you said he might. Stuck his damn nose into our business again. I figure it's time we cut it off."

"Then why didn't you kill him?" Eva asked, and there was no mistaking the viciousness in her voice. Fargo recalled how angry she had been with him when he rejected her advances. She held a grudge, he thought.

"We'll get around to it," Gannon promised. "Thought we might be able to make use of him first, though. We were gonna use him as a hostage in case those redskin lawmen were here when we got back."

Eva waved a hand in disdain. "The Cherokee Lighthorse patrol doesn't know exactly where this place is. With the guards you've posted, they'll never get within a mile of the place without you knowing that they're coming."

Gannon shrugged his massive shoulders and said, "Yeah, I reckon that's right. Still, we thought the old man and the girl might've made it to Tahlequah and asked Howell for help."

"I haven't seen either of them in town," Eva said, and Fargo's heart sank a little. He had hoped that Alma and her grandfather would head straight for Tahlequah. Either they had gone in some other direction, or something had happened to them . . .

Gannon finally let go of Eva and started to turn toward Fargo. His hand closed around the butt of his gun. "I reckon we can go ahead and kill the son of a bitch, then."

"Wait!" Eva said sharply. "Fargo's your prisoner. He can't get away. Maybe it would be a good idea to hang on to him for now, just in case you need him."

"You think so?"

She nodded. "Never throw away a card you might be able to play later."

Gannon snorted. "You been around that fella Kenton too much. You're startin' to sound like him."

Fargo suddenly wondered if there was anything going on between Eva and Matt Kenton. She had Gannon wrapped around her finger, but she wasn't the sort to limit herself to the affections of one man. It was possible that sooner or later she would betray Gannon, too, just as she had betrayed her husband.

But that was Gannon's lookout, Fargo thought. And if it happened, it would serve him right.

Gannon turned to the gang. "Take care of the horses," he ordered. "Dave, you're in charge of guardin' Fargo."

"Sure, Abel," Dave Donaldson said without hesitation. He jerked his gun at Fargo. "Get off that horse."

126

"Put him in the smokehouse," Gannon added. "Nobody's gonna bust out of there."

Fargo slid down from the back of the gelding. Dave came up close behind him and prodded him with the gun barrel. Dave ordered him to go "around back."

The youngster was so green that it hurt. He had made the mistake of getting so close to the Trailsman that Fargo could have spun around, knocked the gun aside, and laid Dave out with a sledgehammer punch, before the young man could react. Under the circumstances, though, Dave's error wasn't going to do Fargo a bit of good. Too many other well-armed men were closeby. If he tried anything, the outlaws would gun him down.

With Dave trailing him, Fargo went along a narrow path beside the cabin. It led around to the back, where a smaller structure was located. Also sturdily built from logs, it had no windows, and the door was thick and solid. The only other way out, besides the door, was a narrow tin chimney. He couldn't make himself thin enough to escape through there, Fargo thought wryly.

As they neared the smokehouse, Dave said quietly, "Look, I don't like this, Fargo. If I could, I might let you go, for the sake of the friendship between you and my pa. But I can't. You know that. I don't have any choice."

"A man always has choices, Dave," Fargo said.

"Not good ones."

"No, maybe not. Sometimes he's got to pick between the lesser of two evils, as the old saying goes." Fargo paused, then added, "If you stack Abel Gannon up against most folks, he's not going to be the lesser of the evils."

"I know that," Dave said miserably. He jerked the smokehouse door open. "But it's too late. I can't help you. Get in there."

As he stepped into the darkened interior of the building, Fargo planted one more seed in the young man's mind. "Some folks say it's never too late to do the right thing."

"I wish I could believe that."

The door slammed shut. Fargo heard Dave drop the bar, locking him in.

Whoever had built this smokehouse had carefully filled all the chinks between the logs. Hardly any light penetrated into the building—most of that came from the chimney and around the edges of the door. If he'd had his Arkansas Toothpick—and a week to work at it—Fargo might have dug or whittled a way out of here. But he didn't have the knife, and he doubted seriously that Gannon would allow him to live for a week as a prisoner. Gannon would get tired of the situation and kill him before that much time had passed.

With a volatile personality like the one the gang leader possessed, Fargo's imprisonment could come to a violent end at any time, with little or no warning. He had to find a way to get out of here, and he had to find it soon.

For the moment, though, he was going to replenish his strength by resting. He sat down on the hard-packed dirt floor and braced his back against the log wall. Closing his eyes, he drew in deep, regular breaths. He needed food, and he hadn't had anything to drink for quite a while. But right now he didn't have any food or water, so he put them out of his mind. His thoughts cleared and his muscles relaxed, and after a while he slept.

When he awoke, there was no way of knowing for sure how much time had passed. The light appeared even dimmer, which might mean that evening was coming on. His stomach was emptier than ever, and his mouth was parched. The outlaws might just forget about him and leave him out here to die of thirst or starvation, whichever came first. Hell, they might even bet on how long he would last, he thought.

They underestimated how stubborn he was. He would last for a long time.

Or maybe he wouldn't have to. He heard the footsteps of someone approaching the smokehouse. Then the person who was coming paused outside the door. With a scrape of wood, the bar was lifted from the brackets that flanked the door. It came open with a squeal of the hinges.

Fargo's eyes narrowed. His guess that it was twilight outside had been right, but after being in the smokehouse all day, even that gray light was blinding to his eyes. As his vision slowly cleared, he saw the figure standing there in the doorway. He thought his visitor wasn't big enough to be Dave Donaldson.

It wasn't. Eva Dupree said, "Hello, Fargo."

10

The delicious aromas of food and coffee drifted to Fargo's nostrils and made his stomach spasm painfully. Eva stepped closer. Fargo saw that she carried a wooden bowl in one hand and a tin cup in the other.

"Before you get any ideas," she went on, "there are two men right behind me with shotguns. Even if you got past me—which you wouldn't—they'd blow you to pieces before you got two steps out the door. So, if you want this food, you'd better not cause any trouble. What do you say?"

"Give me the food," Fargo growled.

Eva bent over and set the bowl and the cup on the dirt floor. She straightened and backed away. Fargo thought she was going to turn and leave, but as he leaned forward and reached for the food, she paused in the doorway.

He paid little attention to her as he picked up the bowl and lifted it to his mouth. There was no spoon, but he didn't need one to eat the thick stew. He drank the liquid and used his fingers to pick up the chunks of meat and the wild onions. Fargo forced himself to eat slowly. He didn't want to wolf down the food so fast that he got sick and lost it all.

He felt strength flowing back into him. When he had eaten about half of the stew, he set the bowl aside for a moment and picked up the cup. Tendrils of steam still rose from the hot, black brew inside it. The coffee was strong enough to float a nail. Fargo sucked down a healthy swallow of it, burning his mouth a little in the process. He didn't care.

"I do like to see a man with an appetite, who appreciates his food," Eva said sarcastically.

Fargo glanced up. She stood there watching him, with her arms folded across her full breasts. Although the light was bad and growing worse, he could see the smug smile on her lips.

"I do appreciate it," Fargo said as he put down the cup and picked up the bowl again. "I wouldn't have figured you for the domestic type, though, Mrs. Dupree."

Her smile went away. "Don't call me that. I don't want to be reminded of that fool I married."

"Fool is right. He probably thinks you love him and are faithful to him."

"I don't care what he thinks. But that's none of your business, Fargo." She again came a step into the smokehouse. "Simon deserves everything he gets. He was making a fortune buying whiskey from that old man and selling it to my people. But did he share any of it with me? No!"

"So you didn't really care about him selling whiskey to the Cherokee. You just wanted your cut of the profits."

She laughed. "That's right. Without Cloudwalker, Simon's business is ruined. It would be better if the old man was dead, and that slut of a granddaughter with him, but I'll take what I can get. He'll never be able to rebuild those stills. The whiskey trade in Indian Territory is ours now, mine and Abel's."

"What happens when you get tired of Gannon?" Fargo pitched his voice loud enough for the guards outside to hear. "Will you double-cross him, too, and throw in with somebody else? Maybe help Kenton take over the whole operation?"

He had to sow these seeds of discord and hope that the guards would carry them back to Gannon.

Eva took another step toward him, her fists clenching in anger. Her eyes seemed to be on fire in the dim light. She was almost close enough so that Fargo could have lunged forward, grabbed her feet, and upended her. But with those scattergun-wielding guards standing by, such a move would only get him killed.

Eva stopped, and a speculative look came over her beautiful, exotic features. In a voice so low that only Fargo could hear it, she said, "Maybe I will double-cross Abel someday, but it doesn't have to be with Kenton. Maybe there's a stronger man around here, a man more suited to my tastes. You think about that, Fargo."

With that, she turned on her heel and stalked out of the smokehouse, leaving Fargo to finish his supper alone. One of the outlaws slammed the door shut and barred it.

Fargo sipped the coffee, thought about what Eva had just said to him, and chuckled. She was a stubborn, determined woman, and she didn't like to admit defeat. She didn't like the idea that any man could resist her charms.

Maybe he could turn that willfulness to his advantage, Fargo thought.

After he finished eating, he dozed again for a while. The sound of voices outside the smokehouse roused him from an uneasy slumber. A man said, "I don't know about this, Mrs. Dupree. Abel told me—"

"I know what he told you. That's why I don't want you to leave. I just want you to go over by that tree and wait there. Keep your shotgun trained on the door, and if Fargo pokes his head out, blow it off. Fair enough?"

Dave Donaldson was standing guard again. Fargo now recognized his voice for sure as Dave said tentatively, "If you're sure it's all right . . ."

"Have you ever known Abel to go against something I wanted?" Eva Dupree asked.

"Well, ma'am, now that you mention it, I haven't."

Fargo felt a surge of excitement as he heard the door being unbarred. Earlier, his purpose in the things he'd said had been twofold: he had wanted to drive a wedge between Eva and Gannon, and he had wanted to work on Dave's conscience. Now he might have a chance to further both of those ends.

The door opened. Eva came in. She lit a match, and she held the flame to the wick of a small candle she carried in her other hand. As the candle flame caught and spread a yellow glow, she shook out the match and dropped it on the dirt at her feet.

As she came closer to Fargo, she reached back and pulled the door almost closed behind her. "I've been thinking about it," she said. "Have you?"

"You mean the idea of me throwing in with you and taking over from Gannon?" Fargo asked.

"That's right."

"You know who I am," Fargo said. "You know I'm not an outlaw or a whiskey smuggler."

"Oh, yes, I know all about the famous Trailsman." Eva laughed softly. "You're something of a hero, Fargo. But every man has his price. There's something that every man wants badly enough to abandon his ideals and step over the line to get it."

"You think so?"

"I know so," she said confidently as she bent to place the candle on the ground. As she straightened, her fingers went to the buttons of her blouse. "And I know your price, Fargo."

She opened the garment, revealing large, bare breasts tipped with dark brown nipples. Fargo had to admit that it was one of the prettiest busts he had ever seen. Eva dropped the blouse at her feet and stood there naked from the waist up. She had taken off her gunbelt before coming into the smokehouse, but the boots and riding skirt she wore, combined with the partial nudity, gave her a striking, almost barbaric appearance. Fargo had to admit that at this particular moment in time, he wanted her.

But that was a purely physical reaction. Fargo's brain was still well aware of how treacherous, how dangerous, this beautiful woman really was. The smile he put on his face as she sashayed toward him, her breasts swaying slightly, was deliberate.

She dropped to her knees in front of him and reached out to rest her hand on his stiffening shaft. "See?" she said. "I told you I knew what you wanted."

"You're damned sure of yourself," Fargo said in a husky voice. The strain in his words wasn't completely feigned. She was having an effect on him. Her hand closed warmly over his erect member.

"No man who has ever had me was able to say no to me afterward," she said boldly. Her deft fingers unfastened the buttons on his trousers and delved inside to free his manhood. As the thick pole jutted upward, she began to stroke it, running her palm up and down along its length.

Her sensuous caresses made him swell even more, until she needed both hands to encircle him. She leaned toward him, her wings of raven-dark hair falling forward to obscure her face. Her tongue darted out, flicked against the head of his shaft, and then began to glide around it. She kissed and licked all over his organ before the wet heat of her mouth engulfed it.

Fargo closed his eyes and gritted his teeth. He hadn't meant for it to go quite this far. Now things would just have to run their course. Considering the maddening skill Eva showed at what she was doing, it wouldn't be too long. Fargo gave himself over to the pleasure, while still keeping one part of his brain alert and apart from what was going on.

Just as he expected, she brought him quickly to a climax. His hips bucked off the ground as his shaft throbbed and spasmed. When he was spent, she gave his shaft a final squeeze and lick, then lifted her head to smile arrogantly at him.

"You see?" she said. "Every man has his price."

And he was about to tell her that she was still a long way from paying his. He hated to hit a woman, but he figured that under the circumstances . . . one quick, clean punch to the jaw would knock her out.

Fargo never got the chance to strike that blow. The door flew open, and a slender shape charged through it into the smokehouse. Fargo caught a glimpse of long black hair flying in the candlelight. Eva gasped and started to turn around and stand up. She ran right into the haymaker that Alma Cloudwalker threw at her.

Alma's fist smacked into Eva's jaw with a sharp crack. Eva flew backward, losing her balance. She landed in Fargo's lap, and was out cold. Instinctively, his arms went around her to steady her.

Alma looked down at them and said, "Get your hands off that bitch's tits, Skye, and put that big old thing back in your pants. We've got to get out of here."

Despite the danger that no doubt hung over their heads, Fargo could hardly keep from laughing.

Instantly, he became more serious. He didn't know where Alma had come from, but he had mixed emotions about seeing her here now. His main worry was that by invading Devil's Den, she had put herself in danger. Now he not only had to get out of here with a whole skin himself, but he had to protect Alma, too.

Although, considering that punch she had thrown, she could do a pretty good job of protecting herself.

Fargo rolled Eva Dupree's limp form off of him and scrambled to his feet, buttoning his trousers as he did so. "There was a guard outside," Fargo said, thinking of Dave Donaldson. "What happened to him?"

"George took care of him."

Fargo frowned. If by "took care of," Alma meant "killed," then Fargo regretted it, for Grady's sake. But it had been Dave's decision to throw in with a bunch of hoot-owls like the Gannon gang.

And right now, he had other things to worry about.

He picked up Eva's discarded blouse and quickly ripped several strips of fabric from it. He used one strip to tie her hands behind her back and another to bind her feet together. Then he tore a bigger piece off the blouse, wadded it, and thrust it into Eva's mouth, using the last strip of cloth to tie it in place.

"Maybe you should have just choked her to death," Alma muttered. "That would have kept her quiet for sure."

Fargo grinned. "I'm not quite that bloodthirsty. Let's go."

They hurried out of the smokehouse. Fargo was full of questions, but they would have to wait.

Lights burned in the windows of the cabin, but no one moved around the place. Fargo and Alma slipped through the shadows under the trees until a voice hissed at them. They stopped, and George Dayton's bulky figure came out of the darkness.

"Alma, are you all right?" he asked anxiously.

"I'm fine," she assured him. "What did you do with the guard?"

"He's tied up and gagged back in the bushes," the Cherokee Lighthorseman answered, and Fargo felt relieved. Dave Donaldson was a prisoner, not a corpse.

"Fargo, are you wounded?" George went on.

The Trailsman shook his head. "Nope, I'm not hit."

"He looked pretty healthy to me when I went into that smokehouse," Alma said.

Fargo didn't want to get into that now. "How many men do you have?" he asked George.

"Captain Howell and the rest of the company are all here. We're going to clean out this nest of snakes."

That sounded like a good idea to Fargo. Gannon and his men were killers. Technically, the Cherokee Lighthorsemen lacked the jurisdiction to deal with non-Indian criminals, but Fargo thought they could stretch a point here since the victims of the gang's crimes had all been Indians.

And here on the frontier, law and order was usually

a rough affair, anyway, with justice triumphing over technicalities.

Fargo, Alma, and George Dayton faded deeper into the woods. They came to the place where George had left Dave Donaldson. Dave was awake and stirring around a little, but tied up the way he was, he couldn't move much. With the gag in his mouth, the only sounds that escaped were a series of muffled grunts.

"This is the man I came to the Nations to find," Fargo told George.

"Really? I'm glad I just knocked him on the head with the butt of a six-gun, then, instead of cutting his throat like I thought about. You want us to keep him alive?"

"If we can," Fargo said.

George nodded. "I'll tell the captain. No guarantees, though, Fargo. Once the real shooting starts, there's no telling what will happen."

Fargo knew that was true. A stray bullet could kill a man just as surely as one that was aimed at him. Dave seemed to be stashed in an out-of-the-way place, though. With luck, he would be safe here.

"What happened to the guards Gannon posted farther out?"

Fargo couldn't see George's face, but he suspected the tribal policeman had a savage grin on his face when he said, "We had to kill them. I reckon they never expected us peace-loving Cherokee to sneak up on them like we were a bunch of Apaches or something."

Fargo hadn't heard any shots. He suspected the outlying guards had all had their throats slashed.

He and his two companions moved on through the thick woods. As they slowly made their way, George whispered to Fargo, "I reckon you're wondering what we're doing here."

"I figured Alma and her grandfather found you after Gannon raided their place."

"That's right. I kind of, uh, modified the captain's

orders and swung back to the south of Tahlequah. I just had a hunch Gannon was still in those parts. When we ran into Alma and old Jefferson yesterday and heard their story, I knew I was right."

Fargo touched Alma's arm. "How is your grandfather?"

"He's all right," she told him. "We left him in Tahlequah when we rode back there to fetch Captain Howell and the rest of the Lighthorse company. We have friends there who will look after him."

Fargo was glad to hear that Jefferson Cloudwalker had survived the attack and the desperate flight afterward.

George picked up the story. "We figured Gannon would head back here to Devil's Den after raiding Jefferson's farm like that. We didn't get here in time to set a trap for him, but we've got him cornered, anyway. When we saw the way that outlaw was guarding the smokehouse, we figured somebody was being held prisoner in there, and you were the most likely person for that to be, Fargo."

"Then Eva Dupree went in there," Alma said, her voice thick with dislike. "How could you—?" With a shake of her head, she stopped herself. "Never mind."

"How could he what?" George asked.

"I said, never mind," Alma grated.

"All right, all right," George said, holding up his hands in a sign of surrender. "But I'm still mad at you for charging in there like that after I told you not to, Alma. You could've gotten yourself killed."

"I didn't," she said.

George and Fargo both possessed the keen senses that allowed them to glide through the shadows and around the tree trunks. After a moment, George said, "I still don't see what Mrs. Dupree was doing with those outlaws. She and her husband must be tied in with Gannon. They're probably helping Gannon get rid of the loot from his robberies."

Fargo shot a glance at Alma. He couldn't read her expression in the dim light, but he sensed what she must have been feeling. Clearly, George didn't know about the whiskey-selling operation that Simon Dupree and Jefferson Cloudwalker had been involved in. Alma would want to keep it that way.

For the time being, Fargo was willing to go along with that. He hadn't made his final decision on what to do about the situation, though.

A few moments later, Captain Ethan Howell stepped out from behind a bush and said, "Fargo? Is that you?"

"It's me, Ethan," Fargo said as he clasped the hand that the Lighthorse captain thrust out at him.

"You always turn up where there's trouble, don't you?"

"It seems that way," Fargo acknowledged.

"You were Gannon's prisoner?"

"That's right."

"He and all his gang are inside the cabin?"

"Except for the ones you and your men have already taken care of," Fargo said.

Howell nodded. "All right. I guess it's time to smoke them out."

"Do you plan on giving them a chance to surrender?" Fargo asked.

"It's more than they deserve, but . . . yes, I'll call on them to surrender. If they don't, we'll start pouring lead into the cabin."

"I thought you meant it literally when you said you were going to smoke them out," Fargo said. "I was about to volunteer for the job."

Howell looked sharply at him. "What do you mean by that?"

"That cabin is solidly built," Fargo pointed out. "The walls are thick enough to stop most bullets. Gannon burned down Jefferson Cloudwalker's cabin. I think he should get a dose of his own medicine."

Howell chuckled and said, "That sounds like a good idea. But a fella would have to be pretty close to throw a torch on the roof."

"Give me a six-gun and a torch and a few minutes to work my way down there," Fargo said. "Then you can call out to Gannon and tell him to surrender. Chances are, he'll tell you to go to hell. If he does, I'll light the torch and throw it on the roof."

Alma reached out in the darkness to touch Fargo's arm. "Skye, that's too dangerous. You'll get yourself killed."

"Don't worry about me," Fargo assured her. "I'll hunker down when the shooting starts."

"It's a good plan," George put in. "If we don't make them abandon that cabin, they're liable to fort up in there and stay for a long time. Who knows how much food and water and ammunition they have."

"All right," Howell said, reaching a decision. "We'll try Fargo's plan. Are you ready?"

Fargo nodded. "I'm ready."

Howell handed him a revolver. Fargo slid the gun into the empty holster he still wore. For now, this weapon would have to do. He hoped he would be able to find his own Colt later, along with his Arkansas Toothpick.

While Howell and George passed the word to the other men surrounding the cabin at the bottom of Devil's Den, Alma stepped closer to Fargo and put her arms around him for a moment. "Thank you, Skye," she said in a half whisper.

He didn't pretend not to know what she was talking about. "Your grandfather and Dupree have to stop what they've been doing," he said, just as quietly. "It's against the law, and it's bad for your people."

She rested her head against his shoulder. "I know. I . . . I didn't find out what Grandfather was up to until after Gannon attacked us at the cabin. After Grandfather and I got away, he . . . he told me what it was all about."

Fargo believed her. He heard the regret in her voice and was convinced it was real.

"I'm not going to say anything to George or Captain Howell," he promised. "But Mrs. Dupree might, just to spite her husband. I don't have any control over that."

"I guess we'll just have to take our chances," Alma said with a sigh. "But that doesn't change how I feel about you, Skye. Thank you . . . for everything."

She lifted her mouth to his and kissed him—it was a hungry, searching kiss that held the promise of more pleasure to come, at a better time and in a better place. For now, that had to be enough.

Captain Howell came back and handed Fargo a piece of a broken branch. Dry grass had been wrapped thickly around one end of it and tied into place. Howell gave Fargo sulfur-tipped wooden matches as well.

"Give us a owl call when you're ready," Howell said. "We'll hold off until then."

"All right," Fargo agreed. "It shouldn't take me more than ten minutes or so to get into position."

Howell shook his hand. "Good luck."

Fargo slipped off into the brush. He wasn't that familiar with Devil's Den, so he had to make his way toward the cabin through a combination of instinct, keen eyesight, and pure luck. Finally, though, he found himself crouched behind a tree trunk, about fifteen feet from one side of the cabin. A small clearing in the brush gave him room to throw the torch onto the roof if it became necessary to do so—and Fargo was convinced that it would. Abel Gannon didn't strike him as the sort of man to give up without a fight.

Fargo cupped his free hand around his mouth and gave the call of a owl, pitching the sound in a deceptive manner so that it seemed to come from several different directions at once. A second later, a gunshot rang out, and Captain Howell's voice shouted, "Gannon! Abel Gannon! Down there in the cabin!"

The wall facing Fargo had one window in it. Instantly, the light in the window vanished as someone blew out the lantern inside the cabin. That was the only response to Howell's shout, however.

The captain called out again, "Gannon, this is Captain Ethan Howell of the Cherokee Lighthorse! The cabin is surrounded! You and your men throw down your guns and come out of there with your hands up, or we'll start shooting!"

This time Gannon replied to Howell's demand. "Go to hell, redskin!" the giant outlaw bellowed. Hard on the heels of his words, gunshots roared and muzzle flame split the night as the men holed up inside the cabin opened fire. They were shooting blindly, their fusillade of lead ripping through the trees. The Lighthorsemen ringing the hollow returned the fire. Gun thunder filled the air.

The battle of Devil's Den had begun.

11

Fargo broke one of the lucifers from the block of matches and ignited it with his thumbnail. As he held it to the bundle of dry grass tied to the makeshift torch, the tree trunk he was leaning against quivered under the thud of bullets smacking into it. The grass immediately caught fire. Fargo waited a second to let the torch start burning strongly. Then he ducked around the tree and flung the torch toward the cabin.

It arched high in the air as it flew toward the cabin. Even over the roar of gunfire, Fargo heard one of the men inside howl a curse as he caught sight of the torch. Fargo saw the torch land on the roof before the deadly hiss of bullets—scorching through the air close to his head—forced him to dive behind the tree again.

He hoped the torch hadn't bounced and fallen off the cabin roof. If that were the case, then they might be in for a long siege.

Within minutes, the Trailsman heard the crackle of flames grow louder. He glanced around the tree trunk and saw flames lifting into the air from the roof. More cursing came from inside. Now that the cabin was on fire, the men inside couldn't extinguish the flames. They had to leave the cabin or stay there and die as it burned down around them.

Fargo drew the revolver from his holster. He was

the closest one to the cabin. He figured he might as well get in on the action.

The shooting from inside the cabin stopped. Angry voices shouted back and forth. The gang was arguing about what to do, Fargo thought. But they had no choice. The entire roof was ablaze now, and the flames were spreading down the outside walls. Time had run out for the outlaws.

Sure enough, a few moments later the door at the front of the cabin burst open. Men boiled out of the opening, and they were shooting again, spraying the woods with lead as they fought for a slim chance of survival.

Most of the outlaws made it only a few feet before they toppled, having been shot through and through by the members of the Lighthorse company. A few of them staggered on a little farther, but then they fell, too. Fargo held his fire, seeing that his help wasn't really needed. The tribal police had everything under control.

However, one worry gnawed at Fargo's brain. He hadn't seen the huge form of Abel Gannon among the outlaws who had made their futile break. Fargo knew Gannon had been inside the cabin with the others; he had heard the giant's stentorian voice coming from inside there only minutes earlier.

Suddenly, with a tremendous crash, the burning rear wall of the cabin came apart. Stumbling through the wreckage came a massive figure. Sparks showered down around Gannon's head and flames licked at his clothes. Gannon bellowed in pain, but he kept moving. He was heading toward the shed where the gang's horses were kept.

If Gannon reached the horses, he might get away. Fargo didn't know how many men Captain Howell had stationed behind the cabin. Most of the gunfire seemed to have come from the front.

Acting with the speed of thought, Fargo dashed out from his cover and shouted, "Gannon!"

The shambling, burning behemoth paused and swung his shaggy head toward the Trailsman. "Fargo!" Gannon roared, and then he rumbled forward, reminding Fargo, for all the world, of a grizzly bear.

If Gannon ever got his hands on him, he might be as dangerous as a grizzly, too.

Fargo fired, the revolver bucking in his hand as he thumbed off the shots. Gannon stumbled but kept coming. His beard was on fire, and the flames threw a hellish light on his hate-filled face.

Fargo tried to avoid the onrush, but Gannon's berserk fury gave him surprising speed. He crashed into Fargo just as the hammer of the gun clicked on an empty chamber. Fargo was borne backward as if Gannon had been a runaway train.

Fargo twisted desperately in midair to keep the huge weight of the outlaw leader from crushing him. Both men landed hard on the ground. Gannon's sausagelike fingers closed around Fargo's throat.

That was about the worst thing that could have happened, and Fargo knew it. Gannon could crush his windpipe within seconds and squeeze the air—and the life—out of him. Fargo got a hand under Gannon's chin and shoved it upward as hard as he could, forcing the man's head back. Gannon's long beard was still burning. Fargo grabbed it and hauled up on it. Gannon screamed in pain as not only did hair come out by the roots, but also the flames seared his face and eyes.

Fargo tore free of the crushing grip on his throat and slammed a knee into Gannon's midsection. He clubbed his hands together and slammed them into the outlaw's jaw. Fargo knew that several of his shots had struck home. Gannon couldn't keep fighting for much longer. Even his great strength would give out as the blood flowed from his body. For Fargo, it was a matter of staying alive until Gannon lost consciousness or died.

Suddenly, in the garish light cast by the burning cabin, Fargo spotted the hilt of his Arkansas Toothpick, which was sticking up behind Gannon's belt. He grabbed the knife, pulled it free, and plunged the long, heavy blade into Gannon's chest, driving it home with all of his strength. A violent shudder passed through Gannon's body, and then he went limp. His arms fell to his sides. Blood bubbled from his mouth as his final breath leaked from him.

Fargo pulled the knife loose and pushed himself to his feet. He felt a little shaky himself, but a couple of deep breaths steadied him.

"Fargo!" George Dayton's voice shouted his name. "Fargo!" The Lighthorseman came running around the cabin. He kept his rifle trained on Gannon as he hurried up. "Is that Gannon? Is he dead?"

"He's dead," Fargo said with a nod. "What about the others?"

"All of them, too," George confirmed. "They never stopped shooting when they came out of the cabin, never tried to surrender. We didn't have any choice but to cut them down."

"No," Fargo agreed, "I don't reckon you did." Now that it was over, the strain of the past few days was beginning to tell on him. A great weariness had him in its grip. He couldn't relax yet, though. Dave Donaldson was still alive—at least, Fargo hoped he was—and so was Eva Dupree. Fargo was confident that the thick walls of the smokehouse had protected her during the ferocious battle. Fargo hoped that if he could get a moment alone with Dave, he could persuade the young man to keep quiet about Jefferson Cloudwalker's illicit whiskey operation.

Eva was a different story. Fargo knew it wouldn't do a bit of good to ask any favors of her. That would just make her more likely to tell the law what her husband and Cloudwalker had been up to.

Not only that, but if Fargo *did* manage to cover up what Cloudwalker had been doing, that meant Simon Dupree would get away with it, too, and that idea rankled Fargo. He didn't see any way of bringing Dupree to justice, though, without also sending the old man to jail.

Things sure did get in a hell of a mess when people gave in to greed and hate and lust, Fargo thought. The "old fella" who had come up with the Ten Commandments had known what he was talking about.

Alma came running out of the woods and threw herself into Fargo's arms. "Skye, are you hurt?" she asked anxiously.

"Just a mite banged up and tired," he told her with a smile. "I'll be all right."

"Thank goodness!" Alma frowned. "What about that woman?"

Fargo knew from the venom in her voice that she was talking about Eva Dupree. He turned to George and said, "We'd better see about Mrs. Dupree. She was tied up in the smokehouse the last time I saw her."

George nodded and started toward the little building. Fargo and Alma followed. Captain Howell came up as well, with a rifle tucked under his arm, and he joined them.

Fargo had pulled the door shut when he and Alma left, but he hadn't barred it. And it was still closed. George now shoved it open and trained his rifle on the interior, just in case. Light from the burning cabin spilled through the opening, illuminating the close confines of the smokehouse.

It was empty, Fargo was shocked to see. Eva Dupree was nowhere to be seen. The only signs that she had been there were the strips of cloth Fargo had used to bind her. They lay on the ground.

Alma gave a half groan. "I knew it," she said. "I knew that evil witch would get loose somehow!"

Fargo felt a mixture of disappointment and relief. He didn't much care for the idea of Eva being on the loose, but at the same time, as long as she wasn't a prisoner, she couldn't incriminate Jefferson Cloudwalker in the original whiskey-selling scheme. Cloudwalker's freedom in return for Eva escaping justice . . .

It was a hard trade, but Fargo was willing to make it.

They reached Tahlequah late in the afternoon of the next day. Dave Donaldson rode along disconsolately behind Fargo, with his hands tied. Dave was a prisoner only temporarily, though. Fargo had found a chance to talk discreetly with the young man and had worked out a deal.

Since the Cherokee Lighthorsemen had skirted the law in driving the Gannon gang out of Devil's Den, Captain Howell was willing to let Dave go in return for his silence about the matter. Dave had also promised Fargo that he would keep quiet about what Jefferson Cloudwalker's real business had been.

Fargo would take Dave back to Fort Smith with him, reunite the young man with his father, and that would be the end of it. Dave swore that he hadn't killed anyone during the short time he was riding with the Gannon gang, and Fargo believed him. Otherwise, Fargo would never have agreed to let him off.

Fargo made it clear, though, that he was going to stay in touch with Grady Donaldson. Dave would be well advised to stay on the straight and narrow. Maybe, Fargo suggested, he should think about marrying Lydia Mallory and finding some honest work. The Butterfield stage line could probably use him—they were always looking for competent station managers. Besides, Fargo had a feeling that Lydia wouldn't mind putting some distance between her and Fort Smith.

All in all, Fargo was satisfied. Eva Dupree had gotten away, as had Matt Kenton and the murderous Barker. But Fargo intended to look up Kenton when he got back to Fort Smith. He figured Sheriff Albin Brown would be interested in Kenton's connection with the Gannon gang. The Cherokee Nation might not legally be able to touch Kenton, but the State of Arkansas could.

And one of these days, it was possible that Fargo might run across Barker. The West, for all its vastness, was in some ways a small place.

Captain Howell headed for Park Hill to report to Chief John Ross. Fargo suspected the captain would leave out some of the details, but that was all right. The rest of the Lighthorsemen, along with Fargo, Alma, and Dave, rode on into Tahlequah.

As they dismounted in front of Lighthorse headquarters, George Dayton said, "That black-and-white horse of yours is over in the stable yonder, Fargo. He'll be glad to see you."

"I'll be glad to see him," Fargo said with a grin. He patted the gelding's shoulder. "This is a good mount, but that Ovaro is something special."

"What about me, Skye?" Alma murmured as she stepped up close to Fargo. "Am I special?"

Fargo put his hand under her chin and smiled at her. "You sure are. Special enough so that you need a good man who's going to be around for a while, not somebody like me who's always drifting on."

She pouted a little. "You sound like you're getting ready to say good-bye."

"That's right. I'm heading for Fort Smith tomorrow with Dave."

"Then there's still tonight," Alma said, brightening up.

"Yeah," Fargo agreed, his smile widening into a grin. "There's still tonight."

Fargo slipped out of the bed in the hotel room early the next morning, while Alma was still sound asleep, with her dark hair spreading out like a cloud around her head on the pillow. She was beautiful . . . and she was smart. He had a hunch that once he was out of the picture, she would realize what a good man George Dayton was. And George was certainly devoted to her. But if it didn't work out between them, there would be someone else.

Fargo just wasn't anywhere near being ready to settle down. There were still too many places he hadn't seen, too many places he wanted to see again.

He dressed and left the room quietly, heading down to the stable to get the Ovaro ready to ride. He wanted to pick up some more supplies, too, once that was taken care of.

But the doors of Dupree's Emporium were closed and locked, Fargo discovered. He didn't particularly want to see Simon Dupree again, but he was curious about whether or not Eva had returned to Tahlequah. It would be a good idea, too, he thought, to have a talk with Dupree and warn him that his foray into the whiskey business was now over. Alma had already promised to make that clear to her grandfather.

Fargo thought that perhaps he had come by too early, that the store just wasn't open yet, but a man passing by on the street paused and asked, "Are you looking for Dupree, mister?"

"That's right," Fargo said.

The man shook his head, and said, "Nobody knows where he is. The store's been closed, locked up, for the past couple of days. Dupree didn't tell anybody where he was going or when he'd be back."

Fargo frowned. "That's odd, isn't it?"

The man grinned. "Naw. White men are all crazy. No offense, mister."

"None taken," Fargo told him with a chuckle.

He went to another store and bought his supplies, including a new hat. The old one had been burned in Jefferson Cloudwalker's cabin. Then he led the saddled Ovaro down the street to Lighthorse headquarters, where Dave Donaldson had spent the night under the eye of a guard. Officially, Dave wasn't a prisoner. Unofficially, the tribal policemen had been more than happy to keep an eye on him until Fargo could take over. They would be glad to see Dave leave, and

George had warned him, in no uncertain terms, to never set foot in the Nations again.

Dave was a lucky man, Fargo thought. He had crossed the line into outlawry, but he hadn't committed any irredeemable acts while riding with the Gannon gang. He had a father who cared about him and a beautiful young woman who loved him. The chance for him to make something of himself was still there— it was ready for him to grasp, if only he would.

George Dayton met Fargo on the porch of the building. "Ready to ride out, Fargo?" he asked.

The Trailsman nodded. "I'm ready."

"I'll bet Alma was really sorry to see you go."

"I didn't tell her I was leaving just yet," Fargo said.

George's eyebrows lifted in surprise. "You didn't?"

"Nope."

"Are you going to?"

"Wasn't planning on it."

George let out a low whistle. "She's going to be mad as a wet bobcat at you, Fargo."

"Probably," Fargo agreed with a grin. "I'll bet that if you went over there to the hotel dining room, you could have breakfast with her in a little while, and she'd tell you all about it."

George rubbed his jaw in thought. "You reckon so?" he asked.

Fargo nodded solemnly. "I reckon so."

"If you think I'm going to thank you for the advice, you're wrong."

"No thanks necessary." Fargo held out his hand. "You're a good man, George. It's been an honor riding with you."

George hesitated for a second, then clasped Fargo's hand. "You're a hard fellow to dislike, Fargo. And I know, because I've tried."

"I'll be seeing you, George." Dave Donaldson had come out onto the porch as Fargo and the Lighthorseman were shaking hands. "So long."

Dave still looked a little downcast, but his hands

were untied now and he perked up some as he and Fargo rode out of Tahlequah. "I never should have come over here to the Nations in the first place," Dave said.

"Remember that," Fargo told him. "It wouldn't hurt to stay out of places like the Ozark Palace, either."

"I'm just going back one more time," Dave said, his voice sounding grim but determined. "To get Lydia and take her from there."

Fargo was glad to hear that. He had worried for a second that Dave meant to have some sort of showdown with Matt Kenton.

And that was exactly what Fargo planned to do himself.

Grady Donaldson threw his arms around his son in a bear hug and then pounded Dave on the back, ignoring the curious looks from the other people in the hotel lobby. "Damn, it's good to see you, boy," he said, his voice thick with emotion. He looked at Fargo. "Skye, I don't know how to even start thanking you—"

Fargo held up a hand. "Then don't start. We're square now, Grady, and I was glad to help out."

"Still, if there's ever anything I can do for you, just let me know."

Fargo nodded and said, "Start off by patching things up with your son. Dave's got some things to tell you, maybe some hard things for you to hear, but he wants to tell you the truth."

Grady looked up at the slightly taller Dave. "Did you get into some sort of trouble over there in the Nations?"

"Bad trouble," Dave admitted. "But it would have been a lot worse without Mr. Fargo here."

Fargo said, "You two sit down and have your talk. Dave, I'll run that errand we talked about."

"I ought to go get her myself," Dave protested.

"Her?" Grady said.

"Consider it one last favor," Fargo said. He would fetch Lydia Mallory and bring her to the hotel so that Dave wouldn't have to go back to the Ozark Palace Saloon.

He left the hotel and walked up the street, turning the corner into the side street where the saloon was located. It was early evening. Night had fallen, but the Ozark Palace probably wouldn't be very busy yet. Fargo wanted to get Lydia out of there and then return later for his showdown with Kenton.

As he pushed past the thick wooden door and went into the saloon, he saw that his plan wasn't going to work out. Kenton was already there, sitting at a table dealing a hand of solitaire, and as Fargo stepped into the room, the gambler glanced up and saw him. Kenton's eyes narrowed, but he didn't seem surprised to see Fargo alive.

Probably because Eva Dupree was sitting beside him wearing a clinging, low-cut dress. Eva must have told Kenton about the battle between the Gannon gang and the Cherokee Lighthorsemen at Devil's Den.

"Skye? Is that you?"

From the corner of his eye, Fargo saw Lydia Mallory stand up at a table where she sat alone, and hurry toward him. He kept most of his attention focused on Kenton, though. Fargo moved slightly so that Lydia wouldn't get between him and the gambler as she came up to him. He didn't trust Kenton not to go for his gun if he saw the chance.

"Lydia," Fargo said quietly. "Listen to me. Dave Donaldson is up the street in the lobby of the Hamilton House with his father. Go to him, right now."

"But . . . but are you sure Dave would want me to—?"

"He wants you," Fargo said. "He's telling the truth about everything to Grady. They're going to work it all out. That includes you, too." He paused for a second and then added, "How would you feel about being the wife of a stagecoach station manager?"

"I'd love it," she said, her voice trembling a little from the depth of the emotion she felt.

A faint smile tugged at the corner of Fargo's mouth. "You might want to suggest that to him, then. Now skedaddle."

"I'm going, Skye." She touched his arm lightly. "Thank you." Then she left.

If he ever wanted to change what passed for his career, Fargo thought wryly, he could maybe find work as a matchmaker. He seemed to be doing a lot of it these days.

Right now, though, he had a much more grim task to complete.

He started slowly across the room toward Kenton and Eva.

Fargo watched Kenton's hands as they slowly, lazily, continued to deal the cards. If those hands dipped below the table, Fargo intended to go for his gun, because that was what Kenton would be doing. He kept an eye on Eva as well, not trusting her, either.

"Hello, Fargo," Kenton said as the Trailsman came up to the table. "Didn't expect to see you back here in Fort Smith so soon."

"I reckon you must not have; otherwise, you'd have taken off for the tall and uncut by now."

"How do you figure that?" Kenton asked coolly.

"I didn't think you'd want to answer to the law."

"For what? I haven't broken any laws in Arkansas."

"Selling whiskey to Indians is a crime," Fargo pointed out.

Kenton smiled. "I didn't do that. Find somebody who can testify that I ever did. I dare you, Fargo."

Fargo's jaw tightened. He supposed that Kenton was telling the truth. Technically, the gambler *hadn't* sold any whiskey to the Cherokee people. Fargo had upset that apple cart before Kenton and Gannon ever got around to putting their plan into operation.

"How about forcing men like Dave Donaldson to go on the owl hoot?"

"I might have made a suggestion to Dave," Kenton said smoothly, "but I didn't force him or anybody else to do anything."

Fargo's frustration grew as he saw the smug look on Kenton's face. It was beginning to look as if the gambler had outfoxed him. He couldn't prove that Kenton had done anything illegal, even though he knew that Kenton had been up to his neck in the depredations carried out by the Gannon gang.

The saloon's rear door opened and a man stepped inside. As Fargo glanced at the newcomer, he knew he still had one card to play in this game.

"Barker will talk to save his own hide," Fargo said. "He'll tell the law that you paid him to ambush me. And he'll spill everything he knows about your connection with Abel Gannon."

Barker was shambling toward the table after coming in from the back, half drunk, from the looks of him. Kenton glanced at him, and for the first time Fargo saw fear in the gambler's eyes. Kenton started to his feet and snapped, "Barker! Get out of here!"

Barker looked up. His eyes widened in shock as he saw Fargo. "Damn!" he yelped as his hand started toward the gun on his hip. "I'll get him this time, Matt!"

Fargo saw Kenton reaching for a gun, too. His left hand darted down and grasped the edge of the table as his right palmed out the Colt on his hip. He turned over the table, shoving it toward Kenton and Eva. Behind him, alarmed men yelled as they dove for cover. The chances were that this wasn't the first gunfight that had ever broken out in the Ozark Palace.

Fargo threw himself to the right as Barker fired. The slug whipped past his head. He fired twice before he hit the floor. Both bullets smashed into Barker's chest and flung him backward. Fargo landed on his side and rolled. Lead chewed splinters from the floor beside him and kicked sawdust into the air.

Kenton cursed as he pushed the overturned table aside and fired again at Fargo. The bullet screamed over the prone Trailsman's head and thudded into the bar. Fargo lifted his gun, thumbed off a shot, and watched Kenton rock back as the bullet struck him. The gambler swayed as a bright crimson flower of blood bloomed on the snowy breast of his shirt. He tried to get off another shot, but his arm sagged as his finger clenched convulsively and the blast went into the floor. Kenton pitched forward onto his face.

Fargo had lost sight of Eva. She rose now from behind the overturned table, her face twisting with hate as she screamed, "Damn you! You've ruined everything!" She thrust a small-caliber pocket pistol toward Fargo. At this range, the little gun could be as deadly as a forty-five.

Before she could fire, a shot rang out from the back door of the saloon. She staggered, having been hit in the side. Turning, she stared at her husband, who stood there with smoke curling from the barrel of the gun in his hand. Fargo had been ready to fire, to kill Eva if he had to, in defense of his own life, but Simon Dupree had beaten him to it.

Eva dropped the pistol, fell to her knees, and swayed there for a second. "Simon . . . ?" she said in a choked voice. Then her eyes rolled up in her head and she fell across Kenton's body, just as dead as the gambler was.

Slowly, with lurching footsteps, Dupree came further into the saloon, not stopping until he stood over the bodies of his wife and her lover with a dull expression on his face. Fargo stood up and went over to him. He took the gun out of Dupree's hand. Dupree didn't resist.

"I had to do it," Dupree said, his voice sounding flat and lifeless.

"Sure," Fargo said. "You saved my life. At least, that's the story you can tell the sheriff when he gets here. It'll sound better than saying you killed your wife because she took up with another man."

Dupree turned his head to look at Fargo. "I . . . I followed her to Devil's Den. I saw her with Gannon. And then . . . to find her here . . . with Kenton . . . You don't know what it's like . . ."

"Thank God for that," the Trailsman said fervently. "When you're finished here, Dupree, I wouldn't go back to Tahlequah if I was you."

Dupree shook his head. "No. No, I won't go back. There's nothing there for me now." He turned, found a chair, and sat down in it, putting his hands on his knees and staring straight ahead.

Fargo didn't say it, but after looking into Dupree's eyes and seeing the devastation of the man's soul, he didn't figure there was much left for Dupree anywhere.

He went to the bar, where the bartender was just climbing back to his feet. All around the room, men poked their heads out from behind overturned tables. The shooting was over; the carnage was complete.

Fargo ordered a drink while he waited for the sheriff. He didn't have Alma, and he didn't have Lydia, but he still had the Ovaro and the call of distant horizons—a call that he would answer for as long as he could, perhaps even until the day he died. Big skies and clean air; the crisp, cold bite of a mountain stream; the sight of an eagle wheeling high through the heavens overhead—these things and others like them would wash away any bitter memories.

Skye Fargo smiled, ready to ride, ready to answer the call.

LOOKING FORWARD!

**The following is the opening
section of the next novel in the exciting
Trailsman series from Signet:**

**THE TRAILSMAN #270
Colorado Corpse**

*Colorado, 1862—
The beauty of the land,
the ugliness of lawlessness and murder.*

Odd. The door to a fancy hotel suite standing half-open like this.

And not a single sound coming from inside.

Skye Fargo stood in the second-floor hallway of the exclusive Mountain View hotel, which was a gilded tribute to the good luck of the locals. While a lot of Colorado boomtowns had gone bust in the past ten years, Mountain View had turned into a prosperous and permanent town thanks to the rich veins of gold-streaked quartz in the surrounding mountains.

This hotel, with its carpeted hall and brocaded wallpaper and elegant French sconces, was a tribute to the good fortune the locals had enjoyed for eight years now. The saloon and dining facilities on the main floor were even more imposing.

Fargo drew his Colt. That probably wasn't the polite thing to do in a place as refined as this, but he didn't care. He sensed something wrong. And he'd survived by trusting his senses.

In addition to the door being half-open and only silence coming from inside, the suite was dark. The only illumination was from the street lamps below, and even that was dimmed because the pale drapes were drawn.

It was near midnight, the time at which he was supposed to meet the mysterious Carlotta Massett, the woman who'd left a note for him saying that she could help keep his friend Curt Cates from hanging for murder three days from now. She claimed she knew the identity of the real killer and asked that he meet her in her suite at midnight.

He inched the door inward. Stepped across the threshold.

"Carlotta?" he said, his voice sounding ghostlike in the silence. "Carlotta?"

He stood in the center of the large living room that was filled with a fireplace, two huge couches, and other furnishings in the heavily decorous Renaissance Revival style, the British style preferred by the wealthy Americans.

A mewing sound came from near his feet. He looked down to see a tiny kitten, one so small it looked as if it could fit into his large palm, craning its neck upward to see the giant hovering above it. The kitten's fur was mostly white except for a few mixed patches of brown and black. It was too dark to see any other detail.

"Hey there, little one," he said. "Where's your mistress?"

The kitten just mewed again.

Fargo decided to look into the bedroom. He expected to find it empty. No way she would've gone to sleep after leaving him that note.

He walked wide of the feline, not wanting to crush her with one of his boots.

The killer had been hiding at the far end of the second floor, in the closet where the maids stored their buckets and mops and dusters.

The killer watched as Fargo entered the room number that had been printed on the note the killer had sent Fargo this afternoon. The note signed as "Carlotta Massett." Whoever the hell that was.

Now the second part of the evening's work would have to get under way. This might prove to be difficult. Many were the tales told of the Trailsman, and if even half of them were true, he was no man to take chances with.

But the deed must be done and done now. No telling how long Fargo would be in the hotel suite before deciding that he'd been duped. And leave.

The killer moved swiftly, surely.

Neither lamplight nor moonlight pressed against the bedroom drapes. The room was cave-dark. The interior of the canopied bed was almost ominous in its black depths.

Fargo found a lantern. He scraped a lucifer against his belt buckle and got the lantern going. Shimmering gold light filled the room with wavering illumination.

More money had been spent on decorating this bedchamber than any twenty men earned in a year. The closet was expansive enough to need double doors. He threw them open, held the lantern inside.

Empty.

Strange. A woman who could afford a suite like this not having at least a few clothes hanging in the closet.

The empty closet reminded him that he'd seen nothing personal at all in this suite. As if nobody was staying in it. As if the hotel maid had just finished getting it ready between guests.

He searched the rest of the room, finding no trace of anybody who might be staying here. He'd been skeptical of the note—it could easily have been a trap—and now he wondered if he'd been stupid to come here in the first place.

He wanted to find the real killer so that his friend wouldn't die. But the real killer obviously didn't want to be found. Had it been the real killer who'd sent the note?

As he started to lift his boot, he felt a slight pressure on the arch of his left foot. The kitten. He set the lantern down on the elaborately carved bureau with its gigantic oval mirror. Then he bent down and picked up the kitten, stroking her head to satisfy her lonely need.

In the lantern light, he saw that the white fur on her left side was spattered with something liquid and dark. He held her closer to the lantern.

No mistaking what it was. Fargo surveyed the chamber. He'd sure missed something important in his search.

The canopy bed. After taking a second inventory of the room with a few quick glances, he realized what he'd overlooked. The canopy bed—underneath. The fancy burgundy-colored bedspread reached the floor. The kitten had crawled beneath it and gone exploring.

Now it was Fargo's turn to go exploring.

He walked to the bed, got down on his knees, and lifted up the bedspread.

He needed a few seconds for his eyes to adjust to the darkness but soon enough he saw where the kitten had picked up the blood. The naked body of a once lovely, now dead, woman faced him. Her eyes had grown enormous in the last horrible moments of her life. Her open mouth shaped a silent scream.

He got up and went to the bureau, got the lantern and brought it back. He wanted a better look at the woman and the situation under the bed.

The sweet-faced but blood-spattered kitten pranced proudly behind him. Whether Fargo liked it or not, he'd made a new friend.

Now that he could see the corpse better, he saw that the killer had beaten her up before killing her. A kerchief lay nearby. He'd probably gagged her so nobody could hear her scream.

He thought he heard something but when he glanced up, he saw nothing. He couldn't see much, anyway. The chamber was three-quarters dark again with the lantern down on the floor.

The kitten sat about a foot from his hand, watching alertly.

He thought about dragging the woman out from under the bed but realized that was unwise. He'd go for the law and show her to them just as he'd found her. He'd kept the note, too. He'd also show them that. Though he'd been here for a time, he hadn't met the sheriff or any of the deputies. His friend said they were bad people who held the town captive. But you couldn't expect a man who was about to hang to have much good to say about the people who wanted to hang him, could you?

The kitten jumped at him suddenly, meaning to be friendly and playful, but knocked over the lantern instead. Fire was the constant enemy of hotels. The lantern spilled some fuel immediately.

Fargo moved quickly. He righted the lantern and felt along the dark stain on the floor. He'd get some water and wash it off.

That was when it happened.

If Fargo hadn't been busy with the kitten, the lantern, and the spilled fuel, he would have heard the footsteps before it was too late.

He would have jerked away from the descending arc of the heavy fireplace poker. . . .

And then he would have jumped to his feet and hurled himself at the person who'd just crept into the room.

But preoccupied as he was with a room literally crawling with distraction, his response was too little and too late. The poker was swung with such force that his instincts for self-preservation were frozen even before they could reach his consciousness.

The wound was so savage and so deep that his blood was splashed against the wall in dark, sticky pieces so heavy and hairy they did not resemble anything that could have come from a human being.

When the killer was sure that Fargo was unconscious, the rest of the work was undertaken. Fast work, accurate work, important work.

No other series has this much historical action!
THE TRAILSMAN

#243:	WEST TEXAS UPRISING	0-451-20504-9
#244:	PACIFIC POLECOATS	0-451-20538-3
#245:	BLOODY BRAZOS	0-451-20553-7
#246:	TEXAS DEATH STORM	0-451-20572-3
#247:	SEVEN DEVILS SLAUGHTER	0-451-20590-1
#248:	SIX-GUN JUSTICE	0-451-20631-2
#249:	SILVER CITY SLAYER	0-451-20660-6
#250:	ARIZONA AMBUSH	0-451-20680-6
#251:	UTAH UPROAR	0-451-20697-5
#252:	KANSAS CITY SWINDLE	0-451-20729-7
#253:	DEAD MAN'S HAND	0-451-20744-0
#254:	NEBRASKA GUN RUNNERS	0-451-20762-9
#255:	MONTANA MADMEN	0-451-20774-2
#256	HIGH COUNTRY HORROR	0-451-20805-6
#257:	COLORADO CUTTHROATS	0-451-20827-7
#258:	CASINO CARNAGE	0-451-20839-0
#259:	WYOMING WOLF PACK	0-451-20860-9
#260:	BLOOD WEDDING	0-451-20901-X
#261:	DESERT DEATH TRAP	0-451-20925-7
#262:	BADLAND BLOODBATH	0-451-20952-4
#263:	ARKANSAS ASSAULT	0-451-20966-4
#264:	SNAKE RIVER RUINS	0-451-20999-0
#265:	DAKOTA DEATH RATTLE	0-451-21000-X
#266:	SIX-GUN SCHOLAR	0-451-21001-8
#267:	CALIFORNIA CASUALTIES	0-451-21069-4
#268:	NEW MEXICO NYMPH	0-451-21137-5

Available wherever books are sold, or
to order call: 1-800-788-6262

The Guns and Gavel Series
by
Spur Award-winning author
Johnny D. Boggs

Spark on the Prairie
The Trial of the Kiowa Chiefs

"A fine snapshot of history."
—Sandra Whiting

"Somewhere Louis L'Amour [is] giving this
young author a nod of approval."
—David Marion Wilkinson

0-451-20912-5

Also in this series:
Arm of the Bandit
0-451-20741-6

Available wherever books are sold or
to order call 1-800-788-6262

Ralph Cotton

JUSTICE 19496-9

A powerful land baron uses his political influence to persuade local lawmen to release his son from a simple assault charge. The young man, however, is actually the leader of the notorious Half Moon Gang—a mad pack of killers with nothing to lose!

BLOOD MONEY 20676-2

Bounty hunters have millions of reasons to catch J.T. Priest—but Marshal Hart needs only one. And he's sworn to bring the killer down...mano-a-mano.

DEVIL'S DUE 20394-1

The second book in Cotton's "Dead or Alive" series. The *Pistoleros* gang were the most vicious outlaws around—but Hart and Roth thought they had them under control....Until the jailbreak.

JURISDICTION 20547-2

Young Arizona Ranger Sam Burrack has vowed to bring down a posse of murderous outlaws—and save the impressionable young boy they've befriended.

VENGEANCE IS A BULLET 20799-8

Arizona Ranger Sam Burrack must hunt down a lethal killer whose mind is bent by revenge and won't stop killing until the desert is piled high with the bodies of those who wronged him.

S909